The Marriage Scam

Robyn C Rye

Published by robyncrye, 2023.

Also by Robyn C Rye

Farnsworth Sisters
Marrying a Rogue
Rescuing Hannah

The Buckingham Sisters
Lady Maggie's Challenge
Layla's Unwanted Husband

The Evans Family
Sometimes Love is not Enough
Still the One
Moving Forward

Standalone
One More Chance
Lady Jayne's Reputation
Third Time's the Charm
Can't Stop Loving You

The Marriage Scam
An Unlikely Match
Searching For You
The Unexpected Suitor
The Lady and the Duke
Starting Over
An Unforgettable Stranger
The Duke's Revenge
The Temporary Wife
Against The Odds
Betrayed
No Good Turn Goes Unpunished
Lady Eloise's Soldier
Lillian's Forbidden Beau
Remember Me
Always Second Best
When One Door Closes
Coming Home to You
Chasing Shadows
Fool Me Once
Deserting Lady Audrey
My Unlikely Saviour
Lies and Deception
A New Beginning
Julia's Second Chance
The Hidden Enemy
The Maiden's Redemption
Miss Elizabeth's Season

Table of Contents

Copyright © 2020 by
Robyn C Rye

Author's Message

THANK YOU FOR JOINING me in telling the story of Charlotte and Lawrence. I hope you enjoyed their story as much as I enjoyed recounting it.

If you loved the book and have a minute to spare, I would appreciate a brief review on the page or site where you bought the book. Reviews from readers like you make a massive difference in helping new readers find stories like The Marriage Scam. Your help in spreading the word is much appreciated.

Thank you!

robynrye.author@gmail.com

Chapter One

"THIS IS HOPELESS! HOW am I supposed to make this dress presentable?" raged Charlotte. Throwing the offending article to the ground, she rose from her seat and paced.

"Charlotte, must you make such a fuss about fixing a dress? Just tack the extra length of lace to the bottom, and it will do," said Emma.

Emma glared at her sister.

"That's all very well for you to say, but I don't see you re-pairing your clothes."

"You know I can't repair my clothes, and besides, mine don't need repairing," said Emma.

"Well, if you shared the money that father gave you, I might have had reasonable clothes that didn't need repairs either."

"Don't be a goose, Charlotte; you know our father would get angry if he thought you were buying material from the money he gives me for clothes."

"He wouldn't notice if you didn't draw his attention to it. Does he think the pin money he gives Mother and me is enough to upkeep the house and dress in quality clothes? He always has enough money when he's at his club, gambling and drinking, but for us, he comes up short every time," she fumed.

"Don't get angry with something you can't change."

"That's fine for you; I'm the one wearing cast-offs from the church poor box."

"Well, that is not my fault," Emma snapped.

Charlotte grimaced. It was Emma's fault. If she stood firm and refused to have new gowns made unless her sister had a new dress, their father might relent and spend money on clothes for her. However, it didn't suit Emma to have her father out of favour, and the new gowns allowed her to go places Charlotte couldn't attend. Lording it over, Charlotte gave Emma a sense of satisfaction. She might be the second daughter, but her face and figure would allow her to make a splendid match with one of the few single dukes still looking for wives. The fewer rivals she had, the better, and although Emma didn't think her sister was much of a threat, moving Charlotte from social outings gave her a sense of satisfaction. When another debutant or chaperone asked after Charlotte, Emma pretended to be distressed by her sister's lack of regard for the social niceties in which the ton participated. She never revealed the real reason for her sister's absence from the balls and soirees Emma attended because she had the sense to realise that the truth would show her in a poor light.

As Charlotte struggled to reattach the lace to the skirt's faded silk hem, she had a sudden urge to rip the material off and give up on the alterations. The problem with removing the extension was that Charlotte had attached it to the bottom of the dress because it was too short. Her ankles would show if she pulled it off, and the gossips and busybodies would declare her to be fast. No matter what she did, it wasn't possible to hide the fact that Charlotte's clothes were cast-offs.

Emma's attire was new and suitable for any function because, if her father had a few pennies to spare, he would give them to Emma. His rule that Emma should not provide the money to her sister, fuelled by his irrational dislike of his elder daughter, meant that Emma had no reason to justify the purchase of clothes for herself and not for her sister.

Charlotte stood and shook out the creases in her dress. Her poorly fitted garment hid the generous swell of her breasts and disguised her trim waist and curvaceous hips. She was taller than her mother or sister, and her long, curly black hair stood in stark contrast to her fair-haired father and sister.

"Are you finished?" Emma asked.

"No, but I've run out of patience. How am I supposed to make this dress wearable? It was on its last legs when I attached the first piece of lace, but without the extra lace, it's too short." Charlotte said.

It galled Charlotte to visit the church to rummage through the poor box for clothes she could use to alter to fit herself, or for material to patch her clothes and add extra length to her current dresses. The first time Pastor Smithers noticed Charlotte searching through the poor box, he assumed she was altering clothes for the poor and less fortunate, but upon seeing her clothing, he realised he was mistaken. The thought that Lord Whitely made his daughter dress in clothes from the poor box distressed the pastor. If he saw her at the church, he pretended he didn't notice Charlotte hunting through other people's cast-offs, and she was grateful for his consideration.

Charlotte's lack of finery was Arthur Whitely's punishment for being different. The man loathed his elder daughter, convinced that Charlotte was proof of her mother's infidelity. Her father accused his wife of taking a lover and placing a cuckoo in his home. Charlotte resembled her mother, but that did nothing to appease the unreasonable man. Denials of unfaithfulness made no sway with her husband. Angered by her husband's treatment of Charlotte, Lady Elizabeth attempted to convince her husband that his eldest daughter was not the by-blow of some other man. However, the man was adamant in his refusal to believe his wife, citing the different appearance of his daughters as his reason for doubt. Defeated, Lady Elizabeth retired from society, taking refuge in her rooms. She rarely ventured out of her room and ate all of her meals on a tray in her room. Charlotte's mother's retreat angered Charlotte, not simply because she became an unpaid servant, but also because her mother's companion cost money that the family couldn't afford.

When Lady Elizabeth retired from society and ceased to take an active role in managing the household, Arthur Whitely dismissed the housekeeper, insisting that Charlotte take over that role. The few servants that the family kept came to Charlotte for instructions. If Emma had helped with the domestic chores, the job might not have been so taxing, but Emma had no intention of doing servants' work. Besides, she told Charlotte she didn't have time for menial tasks with her full social calendar. They left it to Charlotte to scrimp and save so that the family and servants would have food on the table, but she wondered how long she could keep providing the servants with food and a bed without paying them. She hadn't been able to pay the servants in months, and Charlotte knew it was only a matter of time before they left to find more lucrative employment. Who would her father blame when the cook and the butler quit? Charlotte knew the answer to that question, but didn't know how to fix the myriad of problems caused by her father's drinking and gambling habits.

Charlotte's workload increased after the steward left in disgust when it became clear there was no money to pay him. At first, running the estate terrified Charlotte, but as the months rolled on, she kept the fields productive and the tenants fed. Charlotte was a great believer in asking for help, and now she and one old-timer were working together to get the planting and harvesting done. Charlotte feared she was so busy doing many jobs on the estate that she didn't do any of them well, but as no one else stood up to help, she struggled to do her best.

Charlotte sometimes despaired about the state of their finances, and as a young woman, she was not supposed to know how to balance the accounts or worry about making ends meet. Most of the work Charlotte did was delegated to her by her parents. Her Mother's refusal to leave her room and her Father's drinking and gambling left the running of the household and the estate to Charlotte. Without a few loyal servants, the household would crumble.

Chapter Two

BARON ARTHUR WHITELY sat in one of the many padded armchairs placed around the roaring fire. The muted lighting and the fire's ambience relaxed him. The wooden wainscotting and the plush carpets added to the room's opulence, and the discreet servers made the club one of his favourite places. His gaze roamed around the room, and he nodded to some acquaintances. Securing membership at this private club was a privilege reserved for those with the right pedigree.

With the newspaper folded in front of him, he considered his plans for later tonight. For now, Whitely was content with his lot and still had time to find a card game. He had developed a new system that was bound to be a winner, and he needed to win to hold off his creditors for a while longer. With a significant win tonight, he could settle a few of his overdue bills, and with the remaining cash, he could give Emma the money for a new gown. Thoughts of Emma caused his mind to drift to his other daughter. A grimace crossed his face. No amount of appealing to his better nature would make him accept that Charlotte was his daughter. While she had the same colouring as her mother and stature, the likeness was insufficient to convince him that he had fathered the wench. The sooner he got Charlotte out of his house, the better. If his windfall tonight was substantial, he might have enough funds to bribe some ner-do-well to compromise Charlotte, and once she married, he would have no more to do with her. Whitely chuckled at his ingenuity in developing a brilliant scheme to rid himself of the cuckoo in his home. He set his mind to finding a man with pockets to let. It would be better if Charlotte married a cashed-up man, but her plain appearance would never turn a man's head.

When Whitelý glanced up from his paper, his night took a turn for the worse. He had hoped not to meet any of his creditors tonight before he had time to test out his new system. Could he hide behind the paper? The problem with being a member of a gentleman's club was that the doormen and servers would know the whereabouts of all the patrons and could direct others looking for a particular member. With trepidation, he observed a tall, powerful man walking toward him. The man's confident stride caused Whitely to sweat, and he mopped his brow with his kerchief.

"Down in the dumps are we, Whitely?" inquired a deep voice above him. He looked into the eyes of the Earl of Strafford, Lawrence Clayhurst, and sweat broke out on his brow.

"I need to call on you shortly, say tomorrow in the morning? Is ten o'clock too early for a business call, Whitely?" he asked.

Arthur attempted to be calm as he searched his mind for ways to stop the earl from visiting.

"Ah, let me see. Can we postpone until later in the week, Clayhurst? I remember social engagements that need my attention over the next few days," said Baron Whitely. Given time, he was optimistic he could repay the money he owed the Earl. He ran his finger around his collar like his cravat was choking him. The Earl glared at him with distaste.

"Well, you had better cancel those social arrangements. This visit is not a courtesy call. Oh, and just a word of warning: don't indulge in a card game tonight. You can't afford to lose any additional money because you don't have the means to pay off your outstanding bills. If you still have some blunt, it might be time to head home. Rumours circulating in town say that you have not paid your servants for months. Good day to you, sir," said the Earl as he strode off, heading for the exit.

Arthur Whitely's day had just lost all its colour. His stomach rolled, and the sweat dripped along his forehead once again. If Clayhurst called in his debts, it would ruin him. He had nothing left of value to trade. Damn, if only he had access to the girl's dowries, he could pay off his debts with some to spare. He considered approaching the solicitor, who held the money in trust, but rejected the idea. He had tried to access their funds before, but the lawyer almost sneered at him when he refused. The dowries, which had been from the old duke's estate when he passed away, were to be paid to the husband of each of the girls when they married. If he couldn't get his hands on their dowries, it was time to find husbands for his daughters.

Baron Whitely decided to get rolling drunk with his day ruined and the Earl's warning about gambling ringing in his ears. There was no way he was returning home only to have his eldest daughter look at him with distaste. The knowledge that the ton was gossiping about his financial status was worrying. If he wanted to find a good match for his daughters, prospective suitors would shun the girls when they knew he expected them to pay his gambling debts.

His imbibing did nothing to clear his thoughts, and later, when Whitely staggered out, he felt no better than he did at the start of the drinking bout. When he returned home, he knew that Charlotte would stare at him with disapproval, but at least his wife didn't bother him. It had been a long time since his wife fulfilled her duties, both in and out of the bedroom, and while that suited him, it meant that there was no chance to sire a male heir. However, after looking at Charlotte for years, he no longer trusted his wife to bear his offspring. If she had cuckolded him once, what would stop her from doing it again? Her reclusive behaviour was preferable to dealing with her disapproval, and it was easy enough to find a woman to ease his frustrations. That's what he should do now: find a light skirt that would respond to his wishes. He shook his head. A few hours ago, that was a possibility, but at the moment, he only had enough cash to pay a hackney carriage driver.

The conveyance he flagged down was in poor repair, and the stench of unwashed bodies caused his stomach to roil. Life would be so much easier if he had a carriage of his own, but on a losing streak, one night, he lost the carriage and horses in a bet. He remembered coming home in a hackney that night and Charlotte's contempt when she realised he had lost the carriage and horses in a wager. The most concerning aspect of losing the conveyance was that Emma would need to visit her society friends in a hired vehicle.

As he staggered from the carriage, Whitely mumbled to himself. The carriage and Emma's social life would not be high on his list of concerns if Clayhurst called in his markers.

Chapter Three

"MISTRESS CHARLOTTE, we have ladies come to call," said Williams, the butler.

Charlotte rose from behind the large desk. After a quick look at her attire, she grimaced and said, "I am not fit to receive visitors, Williams. You had best tell Emma and ask her to receive the callers."

Williams bowed his head and said, "Very good, Miss."

Williams found it difficult to watch the spoiled second daughter receive callers while ignoring Charlotte's plight. She would call for refreshments, knowing they couldn't afford to waste food on social calls. Charlotte's kind nature and hard work endeared her to the few remaining staff, and they stayed without pay because leaving would have felt like deserting her.

As Williams left the room, a wave of sadness overwhelmed Charlotte. Was she to spend her life in her father's house acting as the housekeeper, the steward, and a maid? When the ladies called, despite the shabby appearance of the home, Emma put on airs, calling for tea and refreshments for the callers. Later, she would regale Charlotte with the gossip from the ladies, without regard for how Charlotte felt about being ignored.

When the visitors left, Charlotte broached the topic of clothes with her sister.

"We must convince our father to give us enough money to buy clothes. You can't wear the same dress to every event you attend, and I can't answer calls because this is the only dress I own. You do well with

Father; why don't you try to convince him we need money for clothes?" said Charlotte.

"If Father comes home early enough, I will broach the topic at suppertime. I don't think he will extend any money. He hasn't paid the staff for a while, so there will be no money unless he wins," Emma replied.

When the girls heard a carriage draw up outside, they listened to see who Williams let in. By the loud, slurred speech, they knew it was their father, and the opportunity to speak to him would not present itself tonight.

"We should look in Mother's dressing room. She had lots of clothes at one stage. Do you think you could alter them?" asked Emma.

"If they're still good, I can, but I shouldn't have to do everything. All I ever do is clean, repair and organise. I'm treated as an unpaid servant here. We are in circumstances that aren't my fault, so why should I carry the burden?"

"My sewing is poor, so it makes little sense for me to repair garments. You would have more time if you organised Betsy to do more cleaning. As the older daughter, your job is to manage the household while our Mother feels unwell."

"How can I make Betsy do more? We haven't paid her in months; we're lucky she's still here. Why don't you supervise the meals? Even if she is well, our Mother doesn't come to join us for meals."

Since her thirteenth birthday, Charlotte had been running the house when her father decided they no longer needed a housekeeper and fired the woman. While Charlotte was now adept at organising the staff, she chafed at having to handle all the duties. The spat was one the girls often had, but no matter how Charlotte pressed her case, Emma sidestepped, taking on more responsibility.

Seated in the withdrawing room, the girls were surprised by a knock at the door. Emma rose to answer it. When she opened the door, Williams was standing outside. "Ladies, your father wants you to join him in his study. He has important news to impart to you," he said with a bow.

"Do you think he had a big win, or will he tell us he lost the house in a card game?" Emma asked.

"I'm sorry, Miss Emma, but I'm not sure," Williams answered.

"Is he sober enough to make any important announcements?" asked Charlotte.

"He has sobered up fast," replied Williams.

When the girls entered the study, their father reclined behind his desk. He glared at Charlotte and said,

"Must you dress worse than the help? That brown garment you are wearing resembles a cast-off bag. You're supposed to be the daughter of the house. If Emma can dress well, the least you could do is try."

Charlotte returned her father's gaze.

"It is a cast-off. The pastor at the church pretends he doesn't see me when I rummage through the poor box. You won't give me enough allowance to buy material, so I have no alternative but to wear this garment."

"Don't be impertinent," her father snapped. "If you made better use of your money, you could dress well enough."

Charlotte clenched her fists, and the words spewed out of her mouth like white-white-hot lava. "That's the point; you give money to Emma, but you never give me any money. Am I supposed to make clothes from thin air?"

Her father rose from his desk and roared, "That is enough! I will hear no more from you!"

He stalked towards her, and for a moment, Charlotte thought he would strike her. She took a step backward. Emma diffused the confrontation when she said, "Father, what of the news you had to tell us?"

The interruption defused the conflict, and he returned to his desk while focusing on Emma.

"Tomorrow morning, I have a visitor coming to see me. The Earl of Stratford will be here, and I want you two to be here if he wants to meet either of you. Will that be too difficult?" he asked his daughters.

"No, Father," Emma exclaimed.

"Then you may go," he said.

Shutting the door behind her, Emma hissed at Charlotte.

"Why do you argue with him? You can't win."

"When he accuses me of dressing worse than the help, he must know that he is the reason. He criticises my attire but won't fund my clothes, so how does he expect me to dress better?"

Refusing to engage in the same argument with Charlotte, Emma said, "I wonder why the Earl is coming tomorrow?"

"Father is probably in debt to the man, and he's coming to take possession of the house. I hope he doesn't want to meet us. If he wants to meet us, you could greet him, and I will stay out of the way. How am I supposed to visit with an earl when this garment, which my father describes as a cast-off bag, is all I own? We'll have to wait and see what happens tomorrow when the earl arrives."

Charlotte wondered why she was the only person in the household who worried about money. Would the Earl throw them out of the house to take possession of the only valuable asset they owned? While her Father drank and gambled, Emma spent money on clothes that could have been spent on bills and food. Her mother reclined in bed, and the wages of her maid could also be diverted if her Mother would take control of the house instead of leaving everything to her.

Chapter Four

CHARLOTTE HEARD THE urgent banging. As she rushed towards the door, the banging continued. Williams opened the door to see a thin boy in grubby clothes. The butler was livid, his speech coming in clipped tones as he said,

"Backdoor for you, son! How dare you come to the front door?"

When Williams went to push the door closed, the boy shouted,

"Mistress Charlotte, ma'am sent me. Lizzy is having the baby, and there is something wrong."

Charlotte hurried into the foyer.

"John, run to the stable and ask Mac to hitch up the horse. I'll meet you outside when I have my supplies."

Charlotte turned to make for the kitchen when Emma grabbed her hand.

"You can't go anywhere; Father instructed us to change to meet the Earl. If you aren't here, he'll be livid."

"Emma, I have nothing to change into, and I can't help it if I miss the Earl. I won't let Lizzy or her baby die on the off chance that the man wishes to inspect us. I'll return as soon as possible," said Charlotte as she collected her basket and rushed towards the front door.

The groom stood at the head of the cantankerous old carriage horse that they used to pull the cart.

"He is fresh, Miss. You will need to be careful," said the groom.

"Thank you," said Charlotte as he assisted her into the cart. The boy clambered onto the tray of the dray, and Charlotte flicked the reins.

The horse took off at a trot with a toss of its head. Charlotte kept the pace even as the horse strained to go faster. A mad gallop to the small crofter's cottage was not a choice. While she was an accomplished horsewoman, she had no hope of holding the horse if it took it into its mind to bolt. Aware that any delay would be a disaster, Charlotte kept her eyes on the road and her mind concentrated on the horse's pace. As the cart approached a bend in the lane, Charlotte gasped and pulled on the reins. The horse threw its head in the air at the sudden attempt to halt it, and the carriage coming towards them took evasive action. Pulling her horse onto the side of the road, Charlotte was incensed to see that the other vehicle's driver barely checked his pace. The conveyance moved at breakneck speed, and the driver shouted a curse at her as he flew past her. Charlotte sat still for a moment, trying to compose herself.

"Please, Mistress Charlotte, my sister needs help. Can we go?" asked the urchin seated on the tray.

Charlotte shook herself and set the horse on its way. The animal was uncooperative, and Charlotte slapped him with the ends of the reins. Ears laid back, the horse kicked out at the flicking reins but moved off as requested.

When they arrived at their destination, a man rushed forward to help Charlotte dismount and take the bridle of the old horse. When Charlotte entered the cottage, the heat was stifling. The number of women in the room for the birth made the heat unbearable. Once she had greeted the worried mother, Charlotte opened the shutters to let in more air and better light. The sixteen-year-old Lizzy lay on a pallet, her swollen belly protruding under the thin material of her shift.

"I need a bowl of water to wash my hands, and you'd better have water boiling on the stove in case I need to sterilise any instruments.

Charlotte approached the terrified girl, stretched out on a pallet on the floor, and smiled in greeting.

"Don't worry, Lizzie. We'll have this sorted soon," she said.

As she ran her hands over the girl's belly, Charlotte could feel the distinct bump that showed the baby's bottom pressed against the girl's pelvis rather than the traditional head-down position. Damn, this birth was going to be tricky. Why had the women waited so long to call her? Surely, they knew by the look of Lizzie's stomach that this birth would be a breach; it was not ideal for a first birth, regardless of the patient's age.

"Martha," she said to the mother, "I need her laid on the kitchen table. Before we lay her down, I want it scrubbed with this soap, but we must be quick."

While the women in the kitchen washed the table, Charlotte took the girl's pulse and monitored the contractions. With the boards cleaned, they moved Lizzy to the table to enable Charlotte better access.

"What will you do, mistress?" asked the mother.

"I'm not sure if we've left it too late, but I will try to turn the baby. It will be uncomfortable for Lizzie, so I have laudanum to give her."

After she gave Lizzie a few drops of the sedative, Charlotte positioned herself alongside the mound of the girl's belly. With her hands cupped around the baby's bottom, Charlotte firmly moved the baby's body. As Charlotte manoeuvred the baby, the women stared, transfixed. Martha stood next to her daughter, all the while wringing her hands. The tension in the kitchen was palpable; all eyes remained focused on Lizzie's belly as Charlotte continued to turn the baby.

Charlotte stepped away from the makeshift operating table and took a large breath.

"We'll give him a minute to rest, and then I'll finish moving him," she said.

As she stepped back to the table, the translucent skin of Lizzie's belly rippled, and the baby rolled itself over.

"Thank God. Now we only have to deliver this little one."

When Charlotte slapped Lizzie gently on the face, the girl became coherent enough to follow her instructions. A first birth was always traumatic for the woman in labour because she had no reference point to tell her how long the pain would last. The effects of the laudanum had long since worn off, and Lizzie moaned and screamed as the woman watched on and Charlotte coached her. When the head and shoulders of the baby slid from the girl's body, the sigh of relief in the room was audible.

"Mistress, we can take it from here if you want to leave."

Charlotte looked over at Lizzie's mother and grinned.

"Not on your life. Cleaning the little person up and having a nurse are the best parts."

Charlotte had been absent from home for nearly three hours but was not in a hurry to return. If the earl hadn't evicted them from their home, Charlotte knew that her input into whatever agreement the men came to would have no bearing on her.

As Charlotte headed the cantankerous horse for home, she prayed that the fool driving the carriage that had nearly run her off the road had continued the journey and wasn't planning to return this way. The joy of delivering Lizzie's baby dimmed a little as she wondered whether the earl had asked to meet her and Emma. The man's desire to inspect the girls was a mystery to Charlotte, but she knew it would infuriate her father if he noted her absence. Surely it was better that the man did not see her, because her ragged clothes and unruly hair would only convince the man that he should seize whatever assets they had before she ran the estate into the ground. He would never know that her appearance did not reflect the efficient way the estate's agricultural operations were run.

Chapter Five

WHITELY ROSE EARLY, his nerves skittering around as he waited for the earl to arrive. If Clayhurst hadn't come when he did last night, Arthur felt sure he could have recouped a large proportion of his losses. He would lose the estate and unentailed properties if the man called in his markers. The shame of having to move to a small cottage would unman him, and the thought of his precious Emma unable to fulfil her destiny made him shudder. The system he devised was foolproof, Arthur thought, and with a win the night before, he would be in a better position to negotiate a settlement with the earl. In hindsight, he realised he should have found a gambling hell before going to the gentlemen's club; he could have tried out his new system, and Clayhurst was less likely to see him.

Williams stood at the door to the study and said, "My lord, the Earl of Stratford has arrived."

"Thank you, Williams. Send him in," said Whitely.

The Earl strode into the room, and Whitely gave him a slight bow. "Please take a seat, Clayhurst. I trust you had a pleasant trip?"

"Do you allow the tenants to drive around on the roads? I nearly collided with a wagon. If the tenants frequent the roads, they should learn how to drive," said the Earl.

"I'm sorry, Clayhurst. I will make inquiries later about the driver's identity."

Seated at the desk, Lawrence Clayhurst looked at Whitely. "You know you have gambled away all your assets and face financial ruin?"

Whitely scowled. "I could pay my debts if the solicitor who has the girl's endowments in a trust fund released the money. The man refuses to consider the idea. As their father, I should be able to access the money that their grandfather left them," Whitely whined.

"It sounds as though the grandfather was a smart man. If the money wasn't in a trust managed by a solicitor and the man released the funds, can you tell me you would not gamble away their dowries? You would lose the money exactly as you have all of your other assets. I don't wish to set your family out in the street or send you all to a pauper's prison; therefore, I will pay out your debts, but I have two conditions."

Arthur Whitely blinked his eyes. His wishes had come true, so he would grant whatever conditions the Earl placed on repaying the debts. Nothing the earl could want could dispel the relief his announcement brought. Arthur Whitely was not stupid; he knew he faced ruin if he didn't pay his debts, but he always thought he was one win away from a windfall. He said,

"Whatever you wish, I'll do whatever you want if you pay my debts."

"You might not be so excited when I tell you my terms. Give up gambling. I will not pay your debts only to see your family thrown off this property in a few months."

Whitely paled and said, "But a man needs a hobby. What will I do with my time?"

Clayhurst gave him a look of disgust. "You could always try running your estate. I hear from the servants that you have abdicated your responsibilities to your eldest daughter. Instead of using your daughter as a steward, hire yourself a responsible man and take control of the land."

The Earl could tell that the choice held no interest for the man, but that was not his problem; he handed the man a life raft. What he did after that was the Earl's choice.

"What is your second condition?"

"I need a wife. I have neither the time nor the inclination to commit to evenings with giggling girls and pushy mamas. One of your daughters will fit the bill."

"Ah, do you wish to meet my daughters?" Whitely enquired.

"No, I have seen them both. The bonnie lass with the blond hair will be suitable."

Arthur Whitely sighed. Just his luck, the Earl wanted to take Emma away, and Charlotte would stay until his dying day. What man wanted a woman dressed no better than a beggar and resembling a beanpole?

Annoyed at the earl's choice, Whitely said, "How do you propose to hold the wedding, Clayhurst? I thought you had business in the Americas. Do you intend to announce your marriage and disappear for four or five months?"

The earl looked down his nose at Whitely.

"Don't be stupid, man! I will send my man of business to present the wedding contracts to you, and he can stand as my proxy at the ceremony."

A kernel of an idea grew in Whitely's mind. If the Earl intended to send a proxy, he'd not see his bride until months after the event. It would be too late for the Earl to renege, and Charlotte would be out of her father's life.

"What is my betrothed's name?"

"Her name is Charlotte," said Whitely. The grin almost appearing on his face would give the game away, so he clamped down on his glee and looked the Earl in the eye.

"Good, I'll send Hildebrand with the marriage contracts. Heed my warning, Whitely; I will not tolerate any news of gambling. If you are accruing gambling debts, I will take you to the cleaners."

Drawing an envelope from his pocket, the Earl handed it to Arthur Whitely.

"See, my wife has proper clothing before sending her to my property. It has been many years since I visited the place, so it will need considerable work to return it to its former glory. A few servants are in residence, and I will inform them of Charlotte's imminent arrival. I wish her to put the place in order before I arrive. Make sure she understands. Good day to you, sir." The Earl left as swiftly as he arrived.

Arthur sat with a grin on his face once the Earl had departed. He had outsmarted the man; the satisfaction of his deception made him chuckle. Why would her father shackle Emma to a man who made his money in trade? Even though the man was an earl, Emma would be a duchess, and no mere earl would thwart Whitely's ambitions for his daughter. Arthur might not be wealthy, but at least he had his pride. The no-gambling condition was tedious, but if it meant he could rid himself of Charlotte, it would be worth it.

Whitely thought of how to siphon off money from Charlotte's dowry. He could contact the solicitor and offer to disperse her funds once the wedding was over. If he told Clayhurst a lower amount, then no one would be the wiser. Whitely smiled; yes, things were looking up. The thought of lining his pockets and getting rid of Charlotte warmed his heart. It didn't hurt that he had bested the damned aristocrat, who thought he had the right to tell Whitely how to live his life.

The thought of telling Charlotte that she was to marry a man she hadn't ever met made Whitely smile. Once she married, he would never need to see her again, and the question of who fathered the girl would be moot. Unfortunately, Whitely had not thought his ruse through because, without Charlotte, all the jobs she did would fall to him.

Chapter Six

CHARLOTTE'S DRIVE HOME was less eventful than her earlier trip. A trip without the horse grabbing the bit and bolting towards its stable was always a good one. The cantankerous horse fought the bit and caused Charlotte anxiety when it shied at a non-existent goblin, but she made it home safely.

When Charlotte reached the house, the stable lad raced out to collect the problematic nag and to help his mistress dismount from the cart. The black carriage that had run her off the road was nowhere in sight, and she felt grateful. Tired emotionally and physically from the stress of the afternoon, all she wanted now was to avoid her father and make it to her room unimpeded.

Charlotte had barely entered the house when Emma confronted her.

"Where have you been?" Emma screeched as Charlotte climbed the stairs.

"Don't be stupid, Emma." Rubbing her eyes, she let out an enormous sigh. "You know full well I was delivering a baby. The Earl has gone, so what is the problem?"

"The problem is that Father has issued a decree that we all need to meet in his office at four o'clock," Emma said.

Charlotte glanced at the timepiece in the entryway. She had fifteen minutes to make herself respectable. Her shoulders slumped, and she ran her hands through the long, curly hair she had tied up at the start of the afternoon. Now, her loose curls spilled over her shoulders and down her back. While protected by an apron, her gown was more crumpled than usual, and she feared there was a smear or two of blood on her skirt.

"Help me pin up my hair," Charlotte said.

The girls raced up the stairs in an unladylike rush, and Emma wielded a brush.

"Blast it, Charlotte; your hair is so thick. Why couldn't you return quicker so we didn't have to rush?"

"I know that you have never concerned yourself with the welfare of the tenants, but when it comes to saving a girl's life and having to rush, there is, for me, no contest. Without my help today, both Lizzy and her baby might have perished. Who would have thought that Father would want us to know what happened in his meeting with the earl? Even though I run his estate, he has never discussed business matters with me."

Thanks to Emma's ministrations, her thick, black hair was bound in a bun, and Charlotte had only a moment or two to straighten her dress before it was time to present themselves to their father's office.

"What manner of mind is he in, Williams? Did the meeting with the earl go well, to your knowledge?" Charlotte enquired.

"Your father is in excellent spirits, considering the earl looked most stern when he left."

Unsure of what to expect, Charlotte asked Williams to announce them. As the sisters entered the room, they were surprised to find their Mother in attendance. The woman sat with her skirts drawn close to herself and her arms crossed. Lady Elizabeth watched her husband warily, and Charlotte agreed with her mother's unspoken worry. Something was amiss when her father requested his wife's presence when making an announcement, and with his apparent good humour, she felt sure that he would deal a deadly blow to one of them. With an uncharacteristic smile, their father beamed at the three women of his family.

"As you know, the Earl of Stratford visited today to conduct business. We have agreed to the terms. He will pay my outstanding debts, and I will give him one of my daughters to become his wife."

The sisters gasped. Their mother rose.

"No, Arthur! Couldn't you devise a better plan than selling one of our daughters?" she said.

"Sit down, woman. It's not as if she will suffer deprivation or abuse. The Earl needs a wife but doesn't want to go through the marriage mart or bother with courting some young chit. So, we agreed Charlotte would suit him well as a wife. During the week, I will have the documents drawn up, and the wedding will take place next weekend."

At the end of his announcement, he beamed at them all. His eyes had a horrid glint as he looked over at his stunned daughter.

"Instead of being a millstone around my neck, you can contribute to the family for once," he said. "If you disagree, I will send Emma, but I doubt she could pull his estate into order. All those years running our estate have been a good training ground for your new role. Clayhurst will send a proxy to the wedding, and then you will travel to his country manor. The Earl will be in the Americas for four months. He expects you to have time enough to get his property running well by the time he arrives," he concluded with a triumphant grin.

Charlotte sat frozen in her seat. The blood roared in her veins, and her breath came in gasps as if she had just run a long distance. Was she to marry an unknown man and move to a ruined estate? How could that be right? For years, she had struggled to make ends meet; this was how her father intended to repay her. Charlotte swallowed, and her stomach lurched. In the stunned silence of the office, her voice quivered.

"Why are you doing this, Father? There must be another way to pay your gambling debts. What about the management of our house and estate? Who will look after their welfare?"

"Clayhurst insists I manage the estate with the help of a steward, and your mother can cease her reclusive ways and take over the running of the house. You are the bane of my life. Make this work because you are not welcome back here if you fail," growled her father. He drew a fat envelope from his jacket pocket and threw it at a surprised Emma.

"The Earl has included money for clothes for you and the servants. He did not want Charlotte to buy new clothes before she left, as he would have clothes befitting a lady of the manor waiting for her when she arrived."

Charlotte crossed her arms and glared at her father. "How is that possible? To the best of my knowledge, he has never seen me. How can he have a wardrobe of clothes ready for me when I arrive? Why would the man leave money for an unknown woman and her servants, who were not in his employ? It would make more sense if the money were for outfitting myself. You have favoured Emma for years, and I wouldn't put it past you to hand her the money that the earl left for me."

Charlotte glanced back at her sister. Emma clutched the fat envelope close to her chest. Whatever the truth about the money, Emma would not relinquish her hold on the cash, and her father would not change his statement. Perhaps marriage to an unknown man would be better than living with her father, who failed to acknowledge her efforts and favoured Emma. If the Earl intended the money for her, would he hold it against her that she did not put it to good use? Surely her husband wouldn't refuse to allow her to buy new gowns?

Chapter Seven

A FEW DAYS PASSED, and her Father smirked at her every time Charlotte saw him. It felt surreal that a decision made by an unknown man could have such a drastic impact on her life. When two distinguished-looking men arrived in a black coach adorned with the Earl's crest, Charlotte realised this nightmare was absolute. The solicitors had the marriage contracts with them. Once her father signed the contracts, Charlotte could not escape the marriage. Her wedding this weekend was a proxy because her betrothed couldn't attend in person.

This state of affairs was a nightmare. Whenever she thought of marriage, Charlotte had hoped that her father might allow her to choose her husband. How could her father expect her to marry a man she hadn't met? Would her father send Emma in her place if she refused to comply? If the earl's estate needed restoring, Emma had neither the knowledge nor the willingness to get her hands dirty, so sending her was not a choice.

At the news of her daughter's impending marriage, her Mother returned to her bedroom. Charlotte attempted to talk to her, but her Mother's abigail sent her away. Her Mother's refusal to speak left Charlotte feeling abandoned. In a few days, she was to go, and everyone else was busy preparing for themselves while leaving Charlotte to fend for herself. Damn them all, Charlotte thought. She would bully her way into the room if she had to force her mother to discuss the situation with her. Determined, Charlotte strode up to her Mother's room.

"I want to see my Mother, Polly," said Charlotte. "You can tell her I am here, or I will barge into her room. The choice is yours."

"Your mam isn't well enough for company," said Polly.

"Well, I'm not company; I am the sacrificial lamb, sold to an unknown man to pay my Father's gambling debts, and I will speak to my Mother."

Charlotte took a deep breath and pushed past the maid. As she opened the door, the stuffy smell of a stagnant room hit her. She strode into the room and opened the windows wide.

"No, miss, you can't do that. Lady Elizabeth suffers from drafts, something dreadful," said the upset servant.

"Go away, Polly," Charlotte said.

The maid, wringing her hands, stood in the doorway.

"It's alright," said Lady Elizabeth. "I will talk with my daughter. Thank you, Polly. You may leave."

Lady Elizabeth raised herself so she could see her daughter.

"I am sorry, Charlotte. The thought that your father had sold you off to a man you've never met distresses me. I hoped my daughters would have love matches, but not something like this," said Lady Elizabeth.

Charlotte's anger boiled over, and she gritted her teeth. Angry words well up in Charlotte's throat. Trying to control her temper, she clenched her fists and stalked from one side of the room to the other.

"If it distresses you, how do you think I feel? Can you not rise from your bed to care for me instead of having the vapours and retiring from life? I am the sacrificial lamb here; I deserve support. My father is sending me into the unknown with nothing more than the dress I stand in, yet Emma is out with Betsy, choosing materials and styles with the mantua maker. I know that the money was for me, but getting my father to admit it is a losing battle. I need more than one dress for the trip. Can you not help me before I leave?"

Despair overwhelmed her, and the tears that had been threatening for days broke through.

"I don't even own a wedding dress. I'm supposed to wear this old rag to my wedding and then for three days in a row for a trip into the countryside," Charlotte sobbed. "There is no way that man has clothes for me at his estate. He considered courting a woman a waste of time, so why would he be considerate enough to have a wardrobe of clothes made for a woman he had never met?"

Charlotte hated to be helpless, but there was no way to influence the overtaking events. Her father smirked whenever their paths crossed. Emma deserted her for the seamstress, and her mother had retired to bed. What was wrong with her family?

Charlotte's despair moved her Mother. She knew what it was to marry a stranger whom you did not grow to care for or respect.

"Help me up, Charlotte. Send Polly to help me dress, and I will see you in the drawing room soon," instructed Lady Elizabeth.

An hour later, the door opened, and Lady Elizabeth and Polly entered the room. Their arms were full of materials and other accessories. For the first time in weeks, excitement surged through Charlotte.

"When I married your father, I had fashionable attire. I know the garments may be out of fashion, but they should still fit and provide you with something to wear on your trip. If the Earl of Stratford hasn't organised clothes for you, as your father said, you will need dresses until he returns."

Charlotte, Polly, and Lady Elizabeth sorted the garments in their mother's dressing room. Once they had chosen six of the most likely dresses, Charlotte retired to her room to try them. Although they needed lengthening, most of the clothes fit because, although she was taller than her mother, they had a similar build. For the first time,

Charlotte felt excited about repairing the dresses she was to wear. The styles, while not in fashion, would look respectable.

"There is one more dress for you to try. Why don't you leave those for Polly to press and freshen up and return to my room?" said her mother.

Laid out on her mother's bed was the most beautiful white dress that Charlotte had ever seen—a silk dress decorated with rows of pearls, with lace on the arms and the hem. The waist of the dress nipped in, and the skirt billowed to the floor. A modestly cut bodice would reveal glimpses of the breasts it enclosed. Charlotte was mute with amazement. She turned to her mother with tears in her eyes.

Her Mother said, "Dear, it's all right. You don't have to wear it if you don't want to. I thought that because we don't have time to make a dress...."

Charlotte interrupted her mother. "Oh, Mother, it's lovely. It would be an honour to wear your dress. Can I try it?"

Lady Elizabeth sighed. "Yes, you can try it. What a pity that your bridegroom won't see you in it. I wonder if he realises how lovely the woman he's marrying is. Are you set for nightclothes? I'm sure the earl doesn't want to see you in a flannel nightgown on your wedding night. Do you have time to make less durable night attire?"

"I have time, but not the material I need. If Emma weren't such a selfish cow, she would offer to help. She is having a wonderful time spending money that I am certain was for me."

"I have a lacy overskirt on the dress I left in the cupboard. Do you want to unpick it and make yourself a nightshirt that his lordship might approve?"

One more task, Charlotte thought, but she was grateful that her mother had roused herself to help. Once Charlotte had unpicked the overskirt, she began the nightgown at her mother's suggestion. When she finished the nightgown, Charlotte turned her attention to the wedding dress.

The white dress needed lengthening, and Charlotte sat late into the night with lace taken from another dress to add to the wedding dress's hem. Her joy at having a wedding dress for the ceremony didn't quell her anxiety, but she felt she deserved some happiness in this sordid arrangement. As the day of the ceremony drew closer, Charlotte became increasingly anxious. What kind of man bartered for a wife and then left the country? Was the need so urgent that the earl couldn't wait the four months before courting her? She feared her usefulness in restoring his estate was the man's motivation, and once she achieved that, would there be a role for her to play in his life? She had spent years serving as a servant and had no intention of letting this unknown earl treat her the same way. The damn man had better treat her with respect and courtesy when they finally met. She didn't know the state of the estate she was supposed to restore to its former glory, but she feared that she had a monumental task in front of her. Despite her concerns, Charlotte had little choice but to accede to her Father's wishes. By the end of the week, she would be married to a man she did not know and sent into the countryside to live.

Her Father and the Earl had used her as a commodity, necessary to clear debts accrued by gambling. Her instructions from the Earl to repair the estate were outrageous. A decent man would supervise the restoration himself, instead of travelling overseas and leaving his new bride to the task.

Chapter Eight

AFTER A HOT BATH, CHARLOTTE sat at the dressing table as her mother's abigail styled her hair. Once Polly finished, she helped Charlotte slide into the wedding dress. Charlotte gazed at her reflection in the mirror, happy with her appearance even though her groom would not be present. Maybe, one day, the proxy would tell her husband how lovely she looked at the wedding ceremony.

"You look lovely, miss," Polly said.

"Charlotte, are you ready?" asked Emma as she entered her sister's room. Charlotte turned towards her sister and heard Emma gasp.

"Where did you get the dress? Father will be furious with you. You should take off that dress and marry in the same dress you always wear," Emma said.

"Why would I want to wear that ill-fitting sack when I can wear Mother's wedding dress? When you marry, will you wear an everyday dress?" Charlotte asked.

"Don't be ridiculous, of course, I won't, but that's different. I won't be making a marriage of convenience to pay Papa's debts. I shall marry the man of my dreams, and I will have a beautiful wedding," replied Emma with a sneer. "Not a hole-in-the-wall ceremony where the bridegroom can't even bother to come."

Determined not to let Emma make her feel second-rate, Charlotte crossed to the door. Just then, her mother arrived with a veil in her hand. The lace veil had a headpiece, like a tiara, and Charlotte felt like a princess for the first time in her life.

"I wasn't sure this would come clean, but Polly has spent the last few days reviving it. Let's put it on; it completes the outfit," she said.

"Mother, this dressing up is ridiculous. Charlotte is marrying a proxy, not the real man. Why go to all this bother? It's not even a proper wedding," Emma said.

Lady Elizabeth smiled at her younger daughter.

"Why don't you tell them we'll be there soon?" she said.

Emma flounced out of the room and slammed the door. Lady Elizabeth smiled at her daughter.

"Your sister is jealous of the attention being paid to you today. She is always the well-dressed woman men want, but you are far more beautiful today. Let us go. Pull the veil over your face; the priest won't ask the proxy to kiss the bride, so that you can leave it there," she said.

Emma walked into the chapel to pass on the message. She walked over to Phillip Hildebrand and sized him up. He returned her appraisal. Yeah, gods, had Lawrence not seen this sister? She was exquisite. Her abigail had styled her blond hair, and her skin was as white and soft as rose petals. The dress she wore enhanced her firm breasts and tiny waist. Phillip's pulse raced as he breathed in her sweet scent.

"So, you, sir, are the substitute?" she asked.

Phillip bowed and said, "Phillip Hilderbrand, at your service. I am the proxy for the Earl."

"Well, Mr Hilderbrand, I must make my apologies for Charlotte. She is wearing my mother's wedding dress as if this were a real wedding," she sneered. "She is making a fool of herself, and I told her so. I said she should wear an everyday dress, but she insisted on my mother's wedding dress. My mother even had the veil cleaned and said it completed the outfit. What rubbish! The dress and veil are a thousand years old. I guess she didn't bother getting a new gown, but there's no way I'll wear someone else's hand-me-downs on my wedding day. I know she is paying off our father's debt, but I couldn't marry a man who didn't take the time to attend the ceremony. I will have no hole-in-the-wall, pretend marriage like this one. My wedding will be grand and celebrated with a huge reception. Charlotte doesn't have a reception; what would be the point without the groom here? And if we left the guest list to her, she would invite the tenants. Charlotte never thought to marry, so she is glad to jump at the chance, even though it's to a man she has never met and can't be bothered to meet her," she mocked.

Phillip reappraised the girl. Her spiteful comments and ridicule of her sister showed a meanness of spirit that diminished her beauty. Had Lawrence seen either of the women? Was Charlotte ugly and set in her ways? From what the sister said, Phillip thought Lawrence had made a monumental blunder, all because he was too busy to court a woman. From his observations, neither of the daughters would make a suitable wife. When the bride entered the room, the sister huffed and took a seat. Phillip couldn't fault Charlotte for wanting to look like a bride; he assumed this was the only time she would be married, so why not make the most of it? Lawrence's announcement that he was going to the Americas for business and needed a proxy surprised Phillip. Even though Phillip knew Lawrence needed a wife to continue his line, it surprised him that the earl didn't postpone the trip and participate in the wedding service. Phillip shrugged; he was a man of business and did as the Duke instructed.

Charlotte and her mother entered the chapel, and her heartbeat was a loud tattoo in her chest. Her father was to give her away, and the irony of the term made her cringe. Her mother kissed her cheek and walked to the front of the chapel to sit next to her sister. Whitely walked towards his daughter and held out his arm. She placed her hand on his arm, and they turned towards the priest. Her future husband's man of business, Hilderbrand, turned to look at the earl's bride. His breath caught in his throat as she walked to the altar with her father. He could not see her face because she wore a veil, but the figure-hugging dress showcased her lithe body. Her black hair, caught in coils, had loose ringlets to soften the effect.

When Charlotte reached the altar, Phillip held out his arm. After a moment's hesitation, Charlotte rested her hand on the proffered arm, but before the ceremony started, Phillip gathered his courage.

"Miss, if you please, will you lift the veil?"

Charlotte hesitated for a moment and then, with shaking hands, grasped the sheer material that covered her face and lifted it up and back behind her head. Phillip now had a view of Lawrence's bride. The younger sister was all glitz and glitter, but this woman was softer, with a warm flush to her cheeks. She eyed him steadily, and he gave her a slight smile. Charlotte momentarily regretted that the man next to her was not the true bridegroom. He treated her with courtesy, and the smile he gave her relaxed her enough to listen to the pastor's words. Hilderbrand turned away from the woman next to him and made his vows without hesitation. When it was her turn, Charlotte wondered what would happen if she refused. She knew she had no choice but to go along with this farce.

When the ceremony finished, the proxy left, and her carriage pulled around to the front of the house. Charlotte was to go straight away, and even though the bridegroom wasn't in attendance, she would have liked a small meal to mark the occasion, but her father would not hear of it. He laughed at her suggestion and said he wasn't spending unnecessary money on her. The footmen loaded her trunks; she only had her goodbyes to say. Charlotte watched in surprise as Emma climbed into the family carriage without as much as a wave goodbye. Even though her husband hurried her, Lady Elizabeth hugged her daughter and wished her well. She never expected well-wishes from her father, but couldn't stop herself from having the last word.

"Father, I hope you have given up gambling; you only have one daughter left to sell off the next time you need to pay your debts. How amusing would it be if you had to sell Emma to an untitled man of low birth?"

Charlotte turned and climbed into the carriage before Arthur Whitely could respond to her barb. One of her husband's footmen closed the door, and she and her newly appointed abigail set off for her new home. It surprised Charlotte that she felt no sadness about leaving her childhood home. What would she miss? A father who spent years criticising her for not resembling her sister, a mother who had been a recluse for so long that Charlotte couldn't remember her any other way, and a sister who was a selfish snob. Her lack of remorse for leaving her home did not alleviate her anxiety about moving to a new one. She counted her blessings for the moment; she had four months to settle in before facing her husband. Her one regret was leaving the tenants and servants to fend for themselves. Neither her Mother nor her sister would care for the tenants and treat their illnesses as Charlotte had, and Williams was too old to find another position, so if things deteriorated, he would lose his home.

Charlotte tried to push her concerns from her mind. There was nothing she could do for those at her Father's estate once she left.

Chapter Nine

THE CONTINUOUS MOTION of the carriage and the punishing pace the driver kept up meant that when they stopped for the night, Charlotte and her maid were both unwell. Despite the rough look of the tavern, the innkeeper's wife accommodated Charlotte's request for a bath and then provided Charlotte with a meal on a tray in her room.

Charlotte hated the outrider's choice of accommodation for the night. The racket from the bar and the giggling in the hallways concerned Charlotte. To what type of establishment had the coach driver brought them? Concerned for her maid's welfare, Charlotte requested that a pallet be brought to her room for the girl.

While they travelled with two outriders, Charlotte didn't think either would rescue her if she screamed.

"Molly, fold the clothes on that chair and lay them at the end of the bed. I am going to put that chair against the door handle. It should stop any intended trespassers in the night."

When they settled for the night, Charlotte lay tensely in the bed, listening to the raucous noise of the patrons in the tavern below. This tavern was not the type of accommodation she had expected, and she guessed the outriders had chosen a place where they could take advantage of the barmaids and drink to excess, with no thought for the women they were supposed to protect. Eventually, fatigue took over, and Charlotte slipped into a restless sleep.

Charlotte woke with a start. The doorknob rattled and shook. When it refused to budge, the intended trespasser cursed. Another voice spoke in the hallway, and Charlotte's heart leapt into her throat. Her eyes narrowed as she concentrated on the sounds outside her door. Sliding from her bed, she nudged the maid with her foot. The frightened girl huddled further under the blankets. Charlotte hissed at her, and she poked her head out from under the covers. Pointing at the bed, Charlotte pulled the girl up and thrust her towards it. She picked up the empty chamber pot and stood behind the door. Her heart pounded, and her breath came in gasps, but determination emboldened Charlotte. If the chair bracing the door gave way, she should be able to hit the first man who entered.

As she listened, a few more curses filtered through the door and someone gave it one last shove. The chair held fast; Charlotte's pulse fluttered wildly. Disgusted, the intruders walked away from the door. Charlotte's shoulders sagged with relief, and she lowered the chamber pot she held above her head. When she returned to bed, tremors wracked her body. She could hear her maid whimpering in her bed, and, to be honest, Charlotte felt weepy too. Too wired up to sleep, Charlotte spent the rest of the night listening to the boisterous laughter and loud, belligerent voices of intoxicated men. Gratified that she had read the situation well, her actions meant she and Molly were safe.

The following day, Charlotte tackled one of the two outriders before they departed.

"Your choice of an inn last night was appalling. Did you forget you are travelling as outriders for the Earl of Stratford's wife, not a light skirt from the slums? Last evening, someone tried to enter my room after I retired for the night, and I know you would not have come to my aid if I had needed help. I assume you chose that place because you knew the barmaids were easy, and you could get drunk and tup them without looking out of place. Your selection for tonight's stopover had better improve on the brothel you had me inhabit last night. I imagine my husband would disapprove of your choice of the inn and would expect you to find lodgings suitable for his wife."

The outrider fidgeted, shuffling his feet as he looked back at Charlotte.

"Ah, yes, my Lady. I will speak to the driver, and we will stop when we reach suitable accommodation," he said.

"Good. Is there any need to travel so fast? You are wearing out the horses, and Molly and I are thrown all over the carriage. Do you move at breakneck speed with the Earl on board?"

"Ah, no, milady, we don't travel so fast with the master on board," said the shamefaced outrider.

"Well, from what I have seen, you have completely disregarded the comfort of your passengers. Do I need to remind you that I am now the Countess, and I expect you to treat me courteously? If you intend to continue in this manner, I will inform the Earl of your behaviour, and I expect you will no longer have a job. Do I make myself clear?"

When the man briefly regarded her silently, she raised her eyebrows at him. He capitulated with a wry grin and bowed as he walked over to talk to the coachman and his fellow outrider.

Molly smiled. "Well done, milady. Those fellows think we're country hicks who don't know any better."

With the accommodation sorted, Charlotte voyaged on through the endless countryside. The coach was moving briskly, but the breakneck speed the driver had used on the first day was absent. While the slower pace meant she and Molly would have to endure being enclosed in the carriage for longer, at least they would arrive with fewer bruises and aches than the fast-paced ride provided.

The further they travelled from the city, the poorer the roads became. Even though the driver had slowed the pace considerably, Charlotte and Molly felt like debris in the sea, tossed wherever the tide took them. The countryside that bordered the road was a monotonous sea of green grass and trees, with the occasional stone fence to break the monotony. When she left her home, it never occurred to her to ask how many days she had to travel to the Earl's estate. Today was their third day in the carriage, but the driver assured them they would soon be on Lord Stratford's land. Charlotte hoped they didn't have to drive for much longer before reaching their destination.

38

Chapter Ten

THE DRIVER SLOWED, and as Charlotte looked out the window, she saw a cluster of houses. People poured out onto the street, and the driver cracked his whip to move some more daring folk away from the vehicle. Charlotte's gaze flittered from the people to their houses. The villagers looked as unkempt as their homes did. Had Claymore abandoned these people without a thought for their welfare? Surely, he could have appointed a steward if he had no interest in his estate?

As the coach slowed further, Charlotte gazed at the neighbouring fields. Most were uncultivated, and she wondered how the estate would survive if the workers didn't plant crops in this prime growing period. With her attention focused on the weed-riddled fields, it surprised Charlotte to hear Molly's quiet exclamation. When she faced the front of the coach, the monstrosity that was the house loomed ahead.

"Good lord!" Charlotte whispered. Wild creepers covered the front of the home, and the front door was barely visible. The driveway was a rutted track, and weeds and thorns covered the turnaround. Large shutters, many of which hung awry, blocked the windows of the house.

The coach drew to a stop, and the driver alighted. As the outriders dismounted, a man emerged from the house. He opened the door of the coach. When he extended his hand, Charlotte had to accept his help to alight from the vehicle.

"Welcome to Clayhurst Manor, milady. I trust you had an enjoyable trip?"

"No, I fear the trip was not enjoyable. Let me introduce my maid, Molly. Who might you be?"

"I am Barrington, and I'm the butler. Let me organise the footmen to carry your trunks inside, and then I will introduce you to the housekeeper."

Barrington manoeuvred back through the partly covered doorway and led them into the foyer. Molly and Charlotte stood in the entry hall as the footmen carried their trunks into the house. As the two weary travellers moved further into the building, Charlotte saw sheets covering furniture in the room closest to the entrance, and discoloured wallpaper was peeling from the walls. The hall table had a thin sheen of dust, and cobwebs hung from the chandelier that dominated the space. Charlotte trailed her finger through the dust and shook her head.

"We appear to have fallen out of the frying pan into the fire."

"Yes, ma'am, you're right."

A woman bustled towards them.

"Welcome, Lady Clayhurst. I'm the housekeeper, Mrs Hatton. Mr Hilderbrand didn't give us much warning of your arrival. Your rooms are clean, and I can ask the cook to prepare a meal for you. Is there something you need?"

"Mrs Hatton, I would kill for a cup of tea and a bath. I believe Molly would second my suggestion. We can drink in the kitchen while the footmen fill a bath. Once we've eaten, we will retire for the night. Could you ask Barrington to stop by when he has the time?"

The housekeeper curtsied and left the room to search for Barrington.

Charlotte rolled her eyes and grimaced.

"Molly, we will be busy ladies for a while. I hope you didn't want a life of luxury as my lady's maid."

"I know how to work hard, Miss Charlotte." She giggled.

"We will have to work like serfs to clean this place before the master arrives."

At the mention of her husband, Charlotte felt shivers run along her spine. The man she had not met would arrive in four months, and she could not pretend he didn't exist then. For now, though, she intended to fulfil her obligation to prepare the house for his habitation and block out thoughts of him.

"Lady Clayhurst, you wanted to speak to me?"

"I did, and as I'm too tired to stand and I don't want to get a crick in my neck, I suggest you take a seat."

Barrington flushed crimson, and Charlotte smiled at him.

"Take a seat, Barrington, and that's an order."

When Barrington seated himself at the table, Charlotte said, "Tell me why this place looks abandoned."

Barrington cleared his throat. "Lord Clayhurst has never lived here, so he did not need to spend time or money on the house's upkeep. He caught us by surprise when his man of business informed us of your marriage."

"How many staff are here?"

"The cook and Mrs Hatton, the footmen and stable hands."

"Are there people in the village we can hire as staff? We cannot get this place ready for his Lordship if we don't get help."

"Yes. The people would welcome employment. Things have been tough for the villages."

"That's another question I have. The houses we saw as we drove through were ramshackle at best; I must confess I've seen better shelters for pigs. The tenants looked both hopeful and angry. What is going on, and why are the paddocks fallow? It is prime growing time; why are there no crops planted?"

"You should speak to the steward, ma'am."

"I will certainly speak to the steward. Once we finish here, I will send someone to deliver a message. Planting the crops is one of the most urgent matters we must fix."

Barrington cleared his throat. "Lady Clayhurst, if you are eager to start the planting, can I offer to send a verbal message to the steward to call at the house?"

"That would be splendid. Ask the steward to call first thing in the morning; I am not one of those ladies who lie in bed until midday; I will be up early. The earl has tasked me with restoring this property to its former glory, which is somewhat ironic considering its current state of disrepair. However, we will do our best; the sooner we start, the sooner we can put things right. Oh, and Barrington, can you try calling me Lady Charlotte? I fear I'm not used to my surname yet, and I may ignore you if it doesn't register."

Barrington nodded. "Certainly, Lady Charlotte.

Once Barrington left, Charlotte calmed her stomach, which had been growling for food for the last hours. The housekeeper provided the much-desired cup of tea and a plate of sandwiches and cold cuts.

"Thank you, Mrs Hatton; that was the remedy I needed. Tomorrow, I will talk with you regarding new staff and menus, but I feel a hot bath waiting."

Chapter Eleven

CHARLOTTE OPENED THE door to her bedroom. It surprised her to find the room neat and clean. The outdated décor was acceptable for the time being. Cleaning the house would be her priority. The bath she had requested sat in front of the fireplace, and the steaming water beckoned her. Molly entered the room and assisted her mistress in unfastening her dress and corset. She lifted Charlotte's chemise off and bundled her hair in a bun.

As the water lapped around her, Charlotte sighed with pleasure. She submerged herself up to her chin and closed her eyes in appreciation. While her mistress bathed, Molly dragged the trunks towards the bed. When she opened the trunk, she groaned. Charlotte rose in the water.

"What's the problem, Molly?"

"There's nothing in your trunk; it's empty."

Charlotte shook her head. Anger rolled in her stomach, and the pleasure she had felt only moments ago dissolved.

"How can it be empty? You packed those dresses I altered, didn't you?"

Molly nodded. "Your dad offered to put the trunk in the coach. I thought he was nice for once. He must have removed everything before he put it on the coach. I'm sorry."

Charlotte sighed. "It's not your fault you credited my father with common decency. Are there clothes in your valise?"

Molly unlocked her trunk. The clothes she packed were still there.

"Well, I will need to share with you tonight. Tomorrow I'll organise a few dresses. I wonder what happened to the clothes my father said the Earl had purchased for me?"

Molly shook her head. "Excuse me if I'm speaking out of turn, but I'll wager your father removed your clothes from the trunk, knowing that the Duke's money was for you. Your father is a wicked man."

"I thought that the money father gave Emma was for clothes for me, but he denied it when I asked him about it. He deliberately gave the money to the wrong sister, and once the envelope was in Emma's hot little hands, she wasn't letting go of it."

"I wondered that. It was peculiar that the Earl gave him money to spend on his staff and his other daughter when he had threatened to call in his debt."

Tears welled in Charlotte's eyes. "I should be used to his treatment, but it galls me. Emma had nice clothes; now she has more, and I still have nothing. I hoped things would change, but even though the location is new, the old clothes and working like a servant have remained the same."

Molly nodded sadly. Charlotte's life at her own home had been challenging, and the remaining servants were sad to see her go, but everyone had assumed that she would be better off with the unknown Earl as her husband. It seemed that their assumptions might be wrong.

Charlotte woke the following day when Molly carried in a cup of tea.

"Cook says that breakfast will be ready in half an hour. That should give us time to refresh the dress you wore yesterday. I'm sure Mrs Hatton will know where to get clothes made."

When Charlotte and Molly headed downstairs, Barrington met them.

"Lady Clayhurst, do you want me to send to the village for girls to help clean?"

"Yes. That would be helpful. Can you send a message to the steward to call us as soon as possible? By looking at the fields, he can't be too busy to see me."

Barrington smiled. "As you wish, Lady Charlotte."

Mrs Hatton provided Charlotte and Molly with a vast array of dishes. It seemed to Charlotte that a smaller breakfast would suffice, as she was the sole resident. When she remembered the tenants lining the road the previous day, Charlotte decided they needed better food distribution. When Charlotte finished eating, she made her way to the kitchen. The cook's name was Pearl, and the woman sat on a seat near the large kitchen table and sipped a drink. When she saw Charlotte, she jumped up, nervously straightening her apron and the skirt beneath it.

"I beg your pardon, Lady Charlotte. Is there something you want?"

Charlotte nodded. "What time did you start this morning, Pearl?"

Pearl flushed. "I started at five this morning to bake the bread; did you want me to start earlier?"

"Good lord, no. I think you should have a break when you need one. I am not running a sweatshop here, so if this drink is your morning tea, please continue the practice. Thank you for your generous breakfast, but I'm not a big eater. If you prepare toast, bacon, eggs, oatmeal, or any other dishes, please only allow enough for me to consume at one meal. I've seen the villagers, and it seems in poor taste to wade my way through a banquet for breakfast when they have so little. Can we meet tomorrow to discuss the dishes? But for now, I want to meet the village girls who have come for a job."

An hour later, Charlotte was busy organising the twenty people who had arrived, hoping to secure jobs. Two girls were to help the cook, and a woman and her three daughters assisted Mrs Hatton with cleaning. The rooms downstairs needed cleaning first, in case ladies from the surrounding estates took it into their heads to welcome the Earl's bride.

Once Barrington and Charlotte assigned the women to their tasks, Charlotte asked Barrington to send one of the stable hands to show her around the house's grounds. She intended to ride the property with the steward, but as he hadn't presented himself yet, she had time to assess the stables and the gardens. The man who arrived at the house to act as her tour guide was nervous about his task.

"James, we might start with the stables and then walk around the gardens."

James nodded and changed direction, walking towards the long, low building that served as the stable block. They were approaching the building when the odour hit Charlotte. Her nose wrinkled, and she pressed her handkerchief over her mouth and nose.

"That is foul! Is this place ever cleaned?"

"Uh, yes, ma'am."

"Who is the stable master?"

"Ah, we don't have anyone, maám."

Charlotte shook her head in despair.

"Tell the men I want to speak with them now."

James disappeared inside the stable block, and minutes later, a grubby group of men stood looking at Charlotte.

"Good day to you all. I need to know if a stable master doesn't organise the work, who does?"

A man muttered. "Ah, we do what we think needs doing."

Charlotte nodded. "That doesn't seem to be working well. Who has been here the longest?"

The oldest of the men stepped forward. "I'm Henry, maám. I've been here for five years."

"Congratulations, Henry. You are now the stable master. I want the horses turned out and the stables cleaned out of soiled hay and bedding today. Create a pile of litter and manure at a distance from the stables. I'll have it removed and placed in the gardens. I want the stable cleaned and the horses back in tonight. Henry, you and I will talk later. Come to the house when you finish. The rest of you, Henry, is in charge. If you disapprove of my decision, speak up now."

Murmurs of assent were the only comments from the men.

"James, you are to go with me."

The gardens showed as much neglect as the rest of the estate, but Charlotte could see where weeds now consumed the original gardens. After years of neglect, mould covered a large fountain, and greenery grew around its base. After walking the perimeter of the grounds, Charlotte's brain buzzed with ideas and plans for reviving the gardens. She felt happy that there was so much to keep her occupied over the next four months. She wondered if her husband was aware of the monumental task he had assigned to his new wife. Surely, if he had never checked on the state of the property after abandoning it, he must have assumed that the task he set his wife was insurmountable. Charlotte shrugged. She would do her best; she could do no more. The only benefit of the situation was that the funds needed for the restoration were not in short supply.

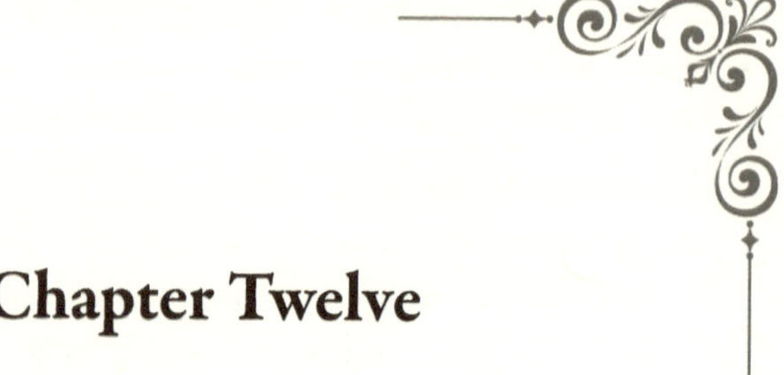

Chapter Twelve

CHARLOTTE SAT IN THE kitchen with Henry. The stables were clean, but Charlotte discovered that no one had been using the horses. There were eight horses and an elderly pony. When Henry told Charlotte about the horses, she frowned.

"Why are there so many horses? Are they favourites of the Earl?"

"No, ma'am. The pony is the horse Lord Clayhurst learned to ride on, and two of them are the carriage horses. The Earl's father bought the others. After he died, the new earl closed up the house and hasn't been back."

"Let's look at them. Are all the horses stabled again?"

"Yes, ma'am, the stables are clean, and the horses are all in their boxes.

As they walked through the stalls, Charlotte checked the horses and asked Henry questions about their temperaments and level of training.

"Guide me here, Henry. The pony needs to go, but what else do you suggest? I want something to ride. We'll need at least two more horses, one for my accompanying groom and one for the Earl if he doesn't bring a horse."

"Well, I agree with the pony, and we need to leave the carriage horses, but we could get rid of the big bay horse and the two smaller greys. If you need something to ride, we should keep the black gelding and the other bay for the groom."

"After the stable is clean in the mornings, get the grooms to work the first three horses. Don't let them ride out until they have worked the horses. We need the pony saddled and led out from one of the other horses, and then we'll see if the village children want him—the others we'll sell in town if we can. Oh, and the horse, for me, needs to get used to a side saddle. Start with a man's saddle, and when you work him down a little, put a side saddle on him."

Henry grinned. "Sounds like you've thought it all out. While the lads work the horses, what do you want me to do?"

After a moment of silence, Charlotte said, "Make a list of the equipment. Once we see what is here, we might sell some of it or send it with the horses we sell. You and the lads can spend all afternoon cleaning tack." She grinned at him, and he chuckled.

"We all love cleaning tack."

As Charlotte ate breakfast two mornings later, Barrington interrupted her.

"Excuse me, Lady Charlotte, the Earl's man of business is here to see you."

Charlotte felt surprised and anxious about Hildebrand's appearance at the property. Was Hilderbrand here to check up on her? Would he think she had overstepped the mark with the plans she had put into practice? Charlotte said, "Show him to, ah, what room is clean?"

"This room is fine, Lady Charlotte," said a deep male voice. Phillip Hilderbrand strolled into the breakfast room and bowed to Charlotte.

"Forgive me for interrupting your breakfast, but the trip was faster than I remembered."

"Phillip, what a surprise. To what do I owe the pleasure?"

"Please don't let me interrupt your breakfast."

When Charlotte seated herself again, Phillip inquired, "May I?" pointing to a chair.

"Of course. Do you want breakfast?

"Yes, please, breakfast would be great. I came to see if you needed help, but this place looks worse than I imagined."

Charlotte grimaced. "When we arrived, I couldn't believe my eyes. We had difficulty getting into the building because a vine almost completely covered the door. What a disaster this place is! I hope you don't think I've overstepped the mark, but the Earl told my Father I was to prepare this place for when he returns."

As he tucked into his meal, Phillip shook his head. "Tell me what you're doing to get this place ready."

"Barrington rounded up workers from the village. Three girls and a mother from the tenant houses are cleaning, and two more girls work in the kitchen with the cook. The stables were a disgrace. Although the men did their chores, no one was overseeing the work. They are now clean, and I appointed a stable master. The stable master, Henry, and I will sell some horses. The grooms are working the horses before saying that they are for sale. There's an old pony that I will give to one of the tenant's kids, and we will put the remaining horses through their paces."

Phillip watched Charlotte's face light up as she discussed her achievements. She had her curly hair pulled back into a bun, but wisps of hair fell around her face. Even though Charlotte chatted excitedly, her voice was warm and energetic. She was unlike any woman his friend Lawrence had dallied with, but having met the sister, he knew Lawrence had chosen the right woman.

"It sounds as though you have everything under control."

"There are two problems that I need help with."

"My dear Lady Charlotte, I am at your disposal. What can I do to help?"

"The steward is refusing to meet with me. I requested him to bring the account books and meet me, but I am still waiting. I've only been here a few days, but I assumed he would respond to my request."

"Why don't we ride over tomorrow to issue that invitation in person?"

"That might work. I'll let Henry know that we'll need two horses."

"Well, that's one problem solved, but you said there were two?"

"The other problem isn't serious; it's more annoying."

"Let me see if I can help."

Charlotte frowned and chewed on her top lip.

"I don't have any clothes, only this dress. Mrs Hatton has asked a tenant to make me a few gowns, but her ability runs to basic clothes suitable for the servant girls."

"What happened to the money Lawrence gave your father for your armoire?"

"My father said the money was for uniforms for the staff and clothes for Emma. I altered dresses that my mother wore years ago, but Father emptied the trunk before I left, unbeknownst to me. I've been using Molly's clothes, but they don't fit."

Phillip growled. "That money was for you to buy clothes. Tarnation, your father is the very devil! He knew the money was for you. Why on earth would Lawrence leave money for your sister and the staff? The idea is ludicrous." He rubbed his jaw. "Lawrence is wealthy beyond belief, so the cost of replacing your garments won't be a problem."

"At the moment, I don't have time to travel to a modiste, and I can't imagine a dressmaker venturing out here. If the seamstress in the village can make me some plain dresses and a nightgown, that will have to do for the time being. The rest of my clothes will have to wait."

Phillip's proclamation that purchasing new clothes for Charlotte would not be a problem made her feel better. Even though she had no time to refurbish her depleted wardrobe, the knowledge that she could do so later cheered her.

Chapter Thirteen

THE FOLLOWING DAY, Charlotte rode around the stable yard on the bay horse she and Henry had agreed to sell. If the horse performed well, they might have to revise their decision. The horse accepted the side saddle without fussing, but Henry was overseeing Charlotte's first ride on the horse. After a few uneventful turns around the yard, he opened the gate to allow her to leave.

As she rode next to Phillip, Charlotte felt a sense of purpose. Today, she intended to see the steward and retrieve the books. She was sure the man had deceived Lawrence, and her sense of decency smarted at the man's dishonesty. Distracted by her thoughts of the steward, Charlotte missed Phillip's question.

"Sorry, Phillip. I was wool-gathering."

"I asked if you wanted to trot. Your mount looks calm. Do you want to pick up the pace?"

Charlotte giggled. "I can tell you've never ridden side-saddle. If we pick up the pace, I need this fellow to canter. I'm game; we'll see what happens when I ask for the canter."

When she tapped the bay with her crop, his head came up, and he took an enormous step. Charlotte reined him in and talked to him in a soft voice. A few moments later, she tried again, and this time, the horse tucked his quarters and led out slowly. With a grin at Phillip, she sat deep and enjoyed the ride. The steward's house was outside the village, and as Charlotte and Phillip rode through the street, the townsfolk's hatred and a sense of helplessness emanated. The sight of the pitiful state in which the women and children were made her angry.

"How could the Earl have abandoned these people without checking that the steward was doing the right job? According to the staff, he let most of the servants go after his Father died and hasn't returned since."

Phillip sighed. "I asked to check the books occasionally, but he had no interest in the estate, but because it's entailed, he couldn't sell it."

The conversation ended as they arrived outside the steward's home. Phillip took in his surroundings. The small cottage that housed the steward had fallen into disrepair. Charlotte let out a sigh and shook her head. "Can you help me dismount, please?"

Phillip hitched his horse to a fence post and returned to lift Charlotte from her mount. The house in front of them looked deserted; had the steward left before she sent him on his way? They approached the house together, and Phillip rapped on the door. A large, unkempt man pulled the door open. He glared at Charlotte and Phillip.

"What do you want?"

"I am Phillip Hilderbrand, the Earl of Stratford's man of business. Phillip stepped forward. Let me introduce Lady Clayhurst. We need to see the accounts, and you can come to the house tomorrow to discuss them."

"What right have you to tell me what to do? I work for the Earl, not you or that woman. I will turn over the books when the Earl requests it."

"Mr White, I am the Earl's wife, and he has directed me to get the estate back to a working farm. We have his permission to take the books, so you should hand them over."

"Not likely."

Phillip smiled. "Give me the books, or I will take them."

White laughed. "A toff like you?"

Phillip advanced and, with little effort, restrained the steward.

Charlotte glared at the man. "You have fifteen minutes to take your belongings; you are no longer the Steward here. Mr Hilderbrand and I will remove the books, and if my guess is right, you'd better leave before we study them. I'm sure the earl will be unhappy at being cheated."

Charlotte sighed with relief as the disgruntled man walked away, his possessions wrapped in a blanket.

"Thanks, Phillip. He wouldn't have given me those books, but I fear they won't make much sense. The tenants said they hadn't planted a crop for years. They are struggling to feed their families. We'll plant crops as soon as I can get them organised."

"That is a splendid idea. Can you organise the men to plant?"

"I'll talk to the farmers and find someone to oversee the seed sowing. There must be a man who knows the rotations and will work with me. We'll do the steward's job between us."

Before taking their leave, Charlotte and Phillip searched the house; she didn't know what she was looking for, but the steward's response to being told to hand over the books was extreme. Did he have something to hide? As she walked towards the back of the small cottage, Charlotte tripped, only catching herself when she grasped the bench.

Phillip smiled. "Clumsy are we, Lady Charlotte?"

Charlotte looked down and noticed she had tripped on a loose board on the floor. She smiled at Phillip.

"Maybe not, my good man. Look at the loose boards here."

Phillip jiggled a plank, and his face became grim when it loosened.

"Look here, Charlotte. Now you know why no one planted crops."

Phillip pulled out another board and removed four bags filled with coins.

"It appears the steward got cocky, believing he had time to steal even more from Lawrence. Good find, Lady Charlotte. As I leave tomorrow, I'll contact the magistrate. If that fellow shows his face around here, we'll have him arrested."

"Do you think he will come back?"

"Wouldn't you if there was a chance that we hadn't found the money?"

As Phillip and Charlotte ate dinner, Charlotte felt pleased with herself. She planned to resurrect the estate, and Phillip approved her decision. She realised she would miss him when he left tomorrow, even though she had servants to talk to, they chose not to speak their minds. Charlotte and Phillip chatted over tea and then retired to the parlour for drinks. It was the most pleasant night Charlotte had had in a long time, and once again, she regretted that Phillip was a proxy, not the groom.

The next day, when Phillip left, Charlotte rode to the village. According to Henry, Thomas was the oldest farmer who knew the planting rotations. Henry introduced Charlotte to Thomas, and she explained her plans. The old man grinned. The opportunity to work alongside Charlotte as the joint steward was one that he would relish.

"If I send the cart for you tomorrow, can you come up to the house to discuss the crops and the preparation needed? We need to get the food growing straight away."

"You'd send a cart for me, Lady Charlotte?"

Charlotte tilted her head towards Henry and smiled.

"I know how to exercise the carriage horses and make the trip easier for the workers. I must convince Henry, but yes, the cart will be here tomorrow."

On the ride back to the house, Henry questioned Charlotte's use of carriage horses to pull a cart.

"We want to keep the horses working, and if you take one of them in the morning to collect the workers and use the other for the return trip, they will both have exercise. It will make the trip easier for the workers, and they won't be tired when they arrive."

Henry scratched his cheek and said, "You want to use the carriage horses to pull the cart? Will his lord approve of that?"

"He may approve or not, but he isn't here, so his opinion doesn't matter. I would think you have enough work exercising the horses in the stable without having to hitch the carriage horses up every few days to maintain their training. If you hate the idea and have a better one, please speak up, and I will consider your thoughts."

Henry grinned. "Seems a bit of a step down for the carriage horses, but it would be foolhardy to break any others in to use on the cart."

"Good; maybe you could teach one of the other stable hands or somebody from the village how to drive, and if you are indisposed, we would still have a driver."

The remembrance of the horse she drove at Westerley, her father's place, caused her to chuckle. When Henry gave her a curious look, she shook her head.

"I can drive a single horse in a cart, but it's probably not the done thing for the lady of the manor to be driving the workers around. At Westerley, I drove a most uncooperative nag who would take it into his mind to bolt without warning. He was the most contrary horse I ever saw, and a good day was when he didn't grab the bit and bolt for home. The carriage horses are better trained and have a better temperament than the unfortunate thing we owned."

"Considering the size of the beasts, I am happy that somebody broke them and trained them on the carriage. The thought of them bolting gives me shudders."

Chapter Fourteen

CHARLOTTE TRIED TO make sense of the books she and Phillip had removed from the steward's house. After she and Thomas had set out a plan for the planting season, she allowed Thomas to allot jobs to the tenant farmers. After the tough times the tenants had endured, Charlotte organised the cook and her helpers to serve a midday meal to the workers. Cook set up large trestles along the main thoroughfare between the house and the stables, and at noon she rang a bell to call everyone in from their jobs. It did Charlotte's heart good to see the workers' appreciation at the feast set out for them each day.

As the weeks passed, Charlotte's changes restored the home to its former glory. Crops were shooting in the fields, and the gardens around the house were taking shape. In the stables, under Henry's direction, everything worked well. With Mrs Hatton's help, Charlotte ransacked the attic, and the lovely old furniture that had sat abandoned for years made its way back into the house. Although parts of the fittings required restoration, the artisans' work was ultimately worth the time it took to complete.

Phillip visited twice more. As the weeks turned into months, his appreciation for Charlotte's work reinforced her decisions. The household settled into a comfortable routine, and the interior glowed from the loving care the extra staff lavished on it. The first temporary workers left, but some had become permanent workers. A glow of satisfaction crept through Charlotte, and her enjoyment at achieving her assigned task grew daily.

The four-month time limit arrived and passed without word of her husband's arrival. Charlotte's emotions see-sawed between nervous anticipation and dread. Her current lifestyle brought her satisfaction, and she hoped the master of the house's return wouldn't disrupt her comfortable life.

As Charlotte and Ben, the groom who had accompanied her on her daily ride, approached the stables, the unusual level of activity caught them off guard. Ben reined in his horse and assisted Charlotte in dismounting after tying her mount to the hitching rail. Henry walked out to meet Charlotte. She scrutinised his face; his expression was grim.

"Lady Charlotte, you have a houseguest."

Her face brightened at the announcement. "I wasn't expecting Phillip, but..."

"It's not Phillip, maám. It is a female friend of Lord Clayhurst."

Charlotte's brows drew together, and her face tightened.

"A lady friend?"

Henry coughed. "Um, she is no lady, maám."

Her nostrils flared, and she raised her chin. "We'll see about that."

Charlotte strode across the yard to the front door with a firm stride. When she opened the door, the chaos that greeted her shocked her into immobility. Trunks blocked the entryway, and Barrington argued with a blowsy blonde woman.

"What in god's name is happening?"

The people in the hallway turned to face her. Barrington's relieved expression would have made her laugh in other circumstances.

"Lady Charlotte, this woman is a friend of the earls. She intends to take up residence until Lord Clayhurst returns."

"From what I have heard, she is no lady." Turning her attention to the woman, she said,

"I assume you have a name."

"I am Mrs Deslie Everton." Her gaze swept over Charlotte, taking in the drab gown and tousled hair. She snickered and held out her hand.

"You must be the little wife."

With her hand remaining at her side, Charlotte said, "You are not welcome here. Remove your trunks and yourself this minute."

The woman smirked.

"I'm sure Lawrence will be furious at you if I leave. A plain little maiden like you will not hold his interest for long. Don't be tedious; give me a room and send a lady's maid to help me. My abigail is unwell and will need to rest."

Charlotte took a step backwards, and in a quavering voice, she said: "Are you telling me that Lord Clayhurst asked you to be here?"

The woman smirked again. "Look in the mirror and see if you need to ask that question."

"Barrington, his Lordship has saddled us with a guest. Find her a room far from me and the earl's room."

With a sly smile, Mrs Everton said, "It would be far better to give me the room with a dressing room and a door into Lawrence's suite. I don't want to roam the hallway during the night."

"Barrington, find her a room far away from Lord Clayhurst." Barrington bowed to his mistress and organised the footmen to collect the trunks strewn at the bottom of the staircase.

Charlotte glared at the woman. "Madam, we will give you a room, and even though your abigail is unwell, you need to manage alone. You are not welcome here; you will eat in your room. When my husband returns, we will sort this out."

Charlotte turned. Most of the household staff were milling around in the hallways.

"People, go back to your jobs, please. Molly, come up to my room, please."

Charlotte entered her room, her head still spinning from her husband's lack of integrity. She shook her head and pressed her hands to her eyes. How could he do this to her? What kind of man had she married? It was bad enough that he had a mistress now that they were married, but how could he humiliate her by expecting her to live under the same roof as the other woman?

"Lady Charlotte, what can I do for you?"

"Molly, can you get the footmen to bring water for a bath?"

The hot water lapped at her shoulders as Charlotte lay in the bath. Tendrils of hair hung around her shoulders even though Molly had tied most of her hair into a ponytail. Left alone with her thoughts, she couldn't decide if she felt angry or upset. While she hadn't entered this marriage expecting love, was it too much to ask for respect? Why couldn't Phillip have been the real groom instead of the proxy? Instead of some unknown man with no sense of decency, she would have had a kind, humorous gentleman who respected her thoughts and discussed the running of the estate with her. A marriage to Phillip would have been harmonious, and Charlotte believed they could grow to care for each other; instead, she had a man who expected his mistress to visit her home. Yeah, gods, she hoped her husband didn't think his mistress could live in the same house as his wife.

When the water grew chilly, she climbed out of the bath. Wrapped in a large towel, she approached the bed. Molly had set out Charlotte's only coloured dress. Charlotte smiled to herself. Molly would defend her like a tigress with her cub; Lawrence's fancy woman didn't stand a chance.

Chapter Fifteen

THE FOLLOWING WEEK crawled past. Now that Lawrence's mistress was in residence, Charlotte assumed the Earl would soon follow suit. She woke each morning with her nerves strung tight, but regardless of when her husband arrived, there were daily jobs that they had to complete.

One afternoon, the sound of hoofbeats filtered through to Charlotte's sitting room. Because no windows looked out onto the driveway, she couldn't be sure who the riders were. As her husband was due within days, the possibility that the visitors were her husband and his men was high. Were her pleasant days going to end?

The thought of meeting the Earl caused Charlotte's stomach to churn, and her heart thumped in fear and anticipation. What kind of man was he? Was he kind or arrogant? The presence of his mistress suggested he did not have a sterling character.

Voices in the hallway showed that Barrington was greeting someone. She waited for him to announce the visitors, but he did not arrive. What should she do? Was there a protocol for meeting one's husband?

Charlotte let him take the initiative, so she re-seated herself and attempted to sew. It was a pleasure to be putting the finishing touches on one of her new dresses. Now that her husband was home, she found it hard to focus. Would he send Barrington to get her or come looking for her himself?

"My Lord, it's good to have you back," Barrington greeted the Earl as he opened the door. Three men followed the Earl into the house."Barrington, you are a sight for sore eyes. We have ridden as though the devil was chasing us for the past three days, and now, we want baths, food, and rest in that order," Lawrence said.

"Excellent, my Lord. Do you wish me to inform the mistress you are home?" asked Barrington.

"No, I have no patience for a scolding wife tonight. With my friends here, we will leave the meeting until tomorrow, when I have rested," Lawrence answered.

One man laughed. Lawrence glared at him.

"What is so amusing, Hilderbrand?"

"I find it funny that you assume your wife is a nag. I can tell you that Mistress Charlotte is a very calm lady," Phillip Hilderbrand said.

"How do you know?" snapped Lawrence.

Phillip laughed again. "Have you forgotten that I married her?" he asked. "I know your wife better than you do. I've visited the house twice a month since the wedding. Barrington, is Countess Charlotte a nag?"

Barrington's eyebrows shot up, and he coughed.

"Ah, no, sir, I do not believe so. It has been a joy to have her here these past months, and she has made remarkable progress in restoring the property." Barrington's face, once blank, showed an exceptional level of animation.

Lawrence glared at his butler and said, "Will you show these gentlemen to their rooms, Barrington? And I want the food prepared while we bathe. Ask her ladyship to have her dinner on a tray in her room tonight; I will see her tomorrow."

When she heard footsteps on the stairs, Charlotte took a deep breath. The steps must belong to her husband, who came to introduce himself to her. A knock on the door sounded, and her heart fluttered, and her pulse raced. After bidding the person enter, Barrington entered the room. Charlotte's shoulder sagged with disappointment. She gave the butler a questioning look, and he said, "My Lady, the master has requested that you eat your meal in your room tonight. He has guests tonight, but will meet with you tomorrow."

Charlotte's face flushed red with humiliation, and she rocked back on her heels. Why was she to stay away from the Earl's guests? Her voice quivered, "Thank you, Barrington. Could you organise a tray?"

Barrington bowed and left the room. He felt uncomfortable telling Lady Charlotte news he knew would upset her. It pained him to know that Lady Charlotte had worked so hard to restore the estate, and her husband didn't have the time to meet her and commend her on her efforts. Why would Lady Charlotte be excluded from dinner? One of the men was Phillip Hilderbrand, and Lady Charlotte, and he had spent many meals together during his visits, so the exclusion seemed futile. Barrington felt confused by the earl's treatment of his new wife.

From her room, the footsteps of the guests as they retired to their bedrooms filtered through to her. Their voices as they talked to one another made her angry. Their footsteps echoed in the hall when they made their way downstairs later. When the maid delivered her food, the noise of rattling cutlery and laughter came to her. This lonely existence had been her life before, with her father banishing her from the dining room at mealtimes. She had eaten on a tray by herself for half of her life. Since arriving at the manor, she ate all meals at the table, whether in the breakfast room or dining room. And she intended to continue her new mealtime routine. Damn the man for his high-handed behaviour.

Charlotte attacked her meal with purpose. Her eyes glittered with anger, and her commitment grew. I will not allow the Earl to banish me from sight, she vowed to herself. And if her husband didn't want to eat together, he could have a tray in his bedroom in future.

As her maid helped her prepare for bed that night, they discovered that someone had locked the connecting door. Molly did not comment, but Charlotte felt her face flush. The man humiliated her twice this afternoon; she hadn't met him yet. Her husband had no intention of consummating the marriage tonight, and relief warred with anger. He had spent four months away, hadn't bothered to make time for the wedding and then banished her to her room when he arrived home.

Charlotte's pulse raced, and her palms became damp as she listened to the sounds of people moving to their bedrooms. When footsteps stopped outside her bedroom door, she held her breath. Had he changed his mind? Would he come into her room? The steps proceeded along the hall, and the breath she held whooshed out of her. Feeling dizzy, she lay in bed, willing her heart to stop its crazy rhythm.

Molly roused Charlotte the following day with the standard tray and the promise of hot water.

"Is my husband at breakfast this morning, Molly?" Charlotte asked.

"I believe he and Mr Hildebrand are out for the day. They told Barrington they would call in at the tavern for food, but they would be back for dinner," Molly said.

Charlotte felt her fists tighten and her jaw clench. The inconsiderate man, her so-called husband, would not spoil her day.

After breakfast, Charlotte set about the tasks that always filled her morning. She kept an eye out as she moved around the estate; she didn't want to run into her husband and his visitors. Charlotte ate her meal alone at lunchtime and then retired to her sitting room to finish the dress she had been working on for the last few days.

When the steady beat of hooves sounded in the driveway, she knew that her husband and his cohorts had returned. It did not surprise her when Barrington knocked on her door. Preparing herself to meet her husband, she smoothed her hair and straightened her dress as she opened the door. Barrington bowed slightly and said, "My lady, the master requests you have your meal in your room tonight."

Charlotte's smile disappeared, and her lips thinned in anger. Her face flushed, and she said to Barrington, "You may tell your master that I will dine alone again tonight, but in the future, if he doesn't wish to dine with me, he will need to eat in his room on a tray. I do not intend to be the invisible lady."

"Ah, yes, my Lady," said Barrington. He turned around so fast that Charlotte didn't see the smile that crossed his face. Barrington returned to the sitting room where the Earl and his associates had seated themselves. He cleared his throat and said, "My Lord, I have a message from her ladyship".

"Well, get on with it then."

"My lord, she wishes you to know that she will once again eat alone in her room tonight, but that in the future, if you prefer not to dine with her, you will need to eat in your room," Barrington relayed the message with a straight face. Phillip Hildebrand hooted with laughter, but the other two men looked mortified.

"Ah, and she wishes you to know that she will not be the invisible lady, sir," he concluded.

"She sent that message, did she? We'll see who gives the orders in this house now that I am home. It sounds like she has gotten too big for her boots while I've been away. Where is my wife's abigail? I need to speak to her."

Phillip continued to grin, and Lawrence glared at him

"What is so damned amusing?"

Phillip chuckled. "You are amusing, Lawrence. Charlotte has had to work hard to get your estate into order, so she is used to doing her own thing. I can't see why you think her an unfit companion at meal times, but I've had many a meal with her, and I can assure you her manners are impeccable."

The conversation ended when Molly arrived, and Lawrence gave instructions for the coming night.

Chapter Sixteen

"MY LADY, THE MASTER, has asked me to prepare you for bed tonight, and then I am to retire," said Molly.

Molly's announcement set Charlotte's nerves racing. She had heard talk amongst the maids, and the action between a man and a woman sounded enjoyable if the man took his time. Charlotte had seen the farm animals mate; surely it couldn't be like that? Would her husband be gentle or take her by force?

Once Molly left, Charlotte waited in her room. The maids had drawn the curtains, and the candles flickered in their sconces. The fire blazed, and while everything looked peaceful, Charlotte's stomach churned. She did not need it spelled out for her. When her husband visited tonight, it would be to consummate the marriage. Her heart pounded, and her palms were sweating. What was she to expect this evening? She knew nothing of what happened in the marriage bed, but not having her mother tell her what to expect left her innocent in both body and mind.

A knock on the door announced her husband's arrival. She was rooted to the spot and unable to find the words to bid him enter. The door opened, and he turned to close it. This visit was her first time seeing him, and she noticed his height. He was a tall, muscular man.

When he turned to face her, she saw the look of confusion on his face. He gazed around the room, and then he focused on her.

"My lord," she said, but he interrupted.

"I do not know what game you are playing, wench, but you need to get out of your mistress's room. Dressed in your chemise can only mean you are here for one thing, but I intend to bed my wife tonight," Lawrence said.

"My lord, you don't understand," Charlotte said.

"Oh, I understand plenty. Wait a few years before you try to seduce a man. How old are you, two or ten years? You have nothing to entice a man. Get out of my sight," Lawrence growled.

"My lord, I am five and twenty years old," Charlotte said.

"Get out!" shouted Lawrence. "And find my wife."

Charlotte's body trembled, and she swallowed the lump in her throat. Her voice quivered as she said, "I am your wife."

Her announcement was like putting a match under dynamite. The Earl exploded. His face was dark and foreboding, brows drawn together, his mouth a hard line.

"What the blazes do you mean? Are you my wife? I didn't ask for a child. The woman I asked for has blond hair and a beautiful countenance. What the dickens are you and your father doing? Is this a scam to land me with his outcast daughter and keep the jewel for a more lucrative marriage?" he shouted.

Charlotte's eyes welled, and she cringed back from the barrage of unkind words and accusations.

"Please, my lord, I didn't know..." Charlotte said.

"You knew, you lying, wench! Get out of my house this minute," he shouted as he opened the door. Grabbing Charlotte, he dragged her out of the bedroom and into the hallway. She was sobbing as he pushed her towards the front door.

"What the devil is going on?" Phillip Hildebrand said as he raced from his bedroom.

"This wench is an impostor; she isn't the woman I wanted to wed. She and her father have pulled a fine scam, and I mean to get rid of her now," Lawrence shouted.

The noise of slamming doors and people shouting had roused half the staff and the guests. Barrington, dressed in a robe, was now in the entryway.

"Phillip, please. Don't let him throw me out in my chemise," Charlotte begged.

Stepping forward, Philip placed a hand on Lawrence's arm. "We need to calm ourselves. You can find the underlying cause of this confusion in the morning. Allow Charlotte to return to her room, and you can sleep on what to do," said Phillip.

The Earl shrugged his friend's hand off his shoulder and said,

"Barrington, unbar the door. Throw this wench out the door."

Barrington flushed a brilliant red and cleared his throat.

"Ah, I'm sorry, my Lord, but I can't let you throw Lady Charlotte out of the house tonight."

"She is not Lady Charlotte; she is an impostor. Do as I say, or I will end your employment," Lawrence yelled.

Charlotte stopped sobbing and, with a hiccupping breath, looked at the Earl with contempt. Her lips curled in a look of disdain, and her chin jutted out as she said, "You, sir, are a worm. You intend to end the employment of someone who has looked after your interests while you jogged around the world, making money and associating with loose women. He may be your servant, but he has decency and integrity, neither of which you have."

Charlotte walked towards Barrington and touched his shoulder. "Open the door, please, Barrington. I will sleep in the stables tonight."

Barrington, his shoulders bowed, said, "Surely not, my lady?"

Transfixed by the events, Phillip only once attempted to involve himself in the drama. His disgust at the scene prompted him to say, "Lawrence, you have taken leave of your senses. Leave this until tomorrow. I fear you will have no staff by morning if you proceed with this stupid action."

Phillip took Charlotte's arm and turned her from the door as Lawrence stood rooted.

"Go to bed, Charlotte. We will sort this out in the morning. Lock the door, Barrington," he continued, "and everyone return to your rooms."

Phillip guided Lawrence to the drawing room and pushed him into a chair. He walked over to the sideboard and collected two glasses and a bottle of the Earl's excellent whisky.

"Lawrence, I realise this has come as a shock, but the staff are fond of Charlotte. Had you persisted with your decision to evict her in the freezing night, they all would have refused to obey. I assume Whitely swapped the girls when you chose to marry by proxy. Is it so awful to be married to Charlotte?" he asked.

"Damn it, man; she looks like she is twelve and has the build to match it. How could any man lust after her, let alone bed her?"

Phillip raised his eyebrows and shook his head.

"Have you seen her in anything but the shapeless chemise? God's teeth, man, you must be blind. On the wedding day, I had to concentrate on the cleric, lest the feel and smell of her next to me make me stumble over the vows," Phillip said.

"Regardless, she is not the wife I wanted. I will ride to the city tomorrow and have a judge annul the marriage. I intend to bring her sister back here as my wife, and that wastrel Whitely won't stand in my way," Lawrence vowed.

"Have you met the younger sister?" Phillip asked.

"No, it matters not. Whitely has not kept his part of the bargain, and I intend to leave tomorrow to rectify the problem," Lawrence said.

"Whitely did you a favour. The younger sister is all glitter and spite. She has an evil nature that she works hard to disguise, but she sometimes fails. Lady Charlotte is sweet but determined. Your estate has never looked better, and the servants are devoted to her. Why not get to know her instead of racing off tomorrow?" Phillip said.

"It won't make any difference. Whitely and the girl pulled a fine scam, and I intend to make them suffer."

"I don't believe Charlotte knew you had asked to wed her sister. Did you meet either of the women? How is it that Whitely scammed you when he used Charlotte's given name? Your focus on making Whitely pay his debts blinded you to the fact that you were dealing with a real person. How could you not know your betrothed's name? Lady Charlotte has turned your estate from a ruined, abandoned farm to a productive estate, and you owe her the chance to explain."

A grunt from Lawrence was the only reply he made to Phillip's comments. Phillip had diffused the situation for now, but who knew what tomorrow would bring? He wondered how Charlotte felt after the unkind tirade Lawrence had shouted at her, and wondered if he had been remiss in not asking Molly to settle her mistress.

Phillip mused over the events of the night. What must Charlotte be thinking now that she knew that Lawrence had not wanted her for his wife, but her sister? After all the work she had done to restore his property, she must feel like she had made a terrible bargain. If Lawrence went through with his threat, the work Charlotte had done would all be for naught.

Chapter Seventeen

WHEN CHARLOTTE WOKE, it was to find Molly readying clothes and toiletries for the day ahead.

"Good morning, Lady Charlotte. After last night's fuss, I thought you would want to look your best for breakfast."

Charlotte's sleep-filled face still bore the remnants of last night's argument. Her eyes were red and puffy, and the dark circles beneath them indicated her lack of sleep. She gave her head a quick shake.

"No, I will have a tray in my room. I cannot survive another barrage from that rude man I married."

Molly set her lips in a thin line.

"If you don't go to breakfast, you leave the field wide open for Mrs Everton. She went to breakfast five minutes ago and will have sweet-talked the earl into swapping rooms with you by now."

Charlotte let out a gasp as she grabbed her undergarments. "Here, help me get ready, Molly. Until his lordship travels to London to have our vows annulled, I am still the mistress of this house."

As Charlotte approached the breakfast room door, Barrington swung into action and opened the door for her. On entering the room, she saw that Molly was correct. Mrs Everton had cozied up against the earl, and Phillip sat at the other end of the table, glaring at the couple.

Phillip rose and moved to greet her, and then pulled out a chair so she could sit.

She smiled at him. "Thank you, Phillip, but I need to sort out a problem, and I'd prefer to stand for the moment."

Charlotte swung around, and her gaze fell on her husband.

"Sir, no husband I am acquainted with would humiliate his wife by having her sleep under the same roof as his mistress. I have had to endure your fancy woman's presence in my home since you brought her here. I will not sit at the table with her, and I am not the one leaving. Until you get an annulment, I am the lady of the house, and you will remove that trollop forthwith."

Lawrence smirked at Charlotte. "If I send Deslie away, will you see to my needs?"

Charlotte's face heated, and she knew she had gone bright red. Phillip rose to come to her aid, but she waved him away.

"If I recall, my lord, you were the one who was unable to fulfil your duties last night."

Charlotte could hear Barrington behind her snort, and she levelled her eyes at her husband.

Lawrence glared at Charlotte. "It's not my fault if your boyish figure doesn't appeal to me."

"Your horrid nature doesn't appeal to me either, so we are at an impasse. But this doesn't change the fact that the woman must go."

Charlotte turned her attention to Barrington.

"Barrington, Mrs Everton needs to change her gown. Please ask Molly to accompany her to the room and assist her in packing her trunks. Tell the stables that the carriage should be ready to leave in half an hour."

"Yes, milady."

Mrs Everton laughed. "There is only one problem with your plan; my lady, I do not need to change my clothes."

With a sweet smile at her adversary, Charlotte walked to the sideboard and picked up an enormous vase. She emptied the flowers from the vessel and hurled the contents at the other woman. A loud screech and profanities spewed from the woman's mouth as the water drenched her.

"It looks as though you were mistaken; you need to change. Oh, dear, Barrington, these flowers need water." He laughed when she winked at him and walked away to do her bidding.

Phillip struggled to control his laugh as he watched the byplay between Charlotte and her rival. Mrs Everton's coiffure was messy, and water ran down her neck to her ample bosom. She stood next to Lawrence and pouted.

"Are you going to let the little tramp treat me like this? I have never been so outraged in my life. Tell the woman I am to stay, Lawrence."

Lawrence glanced at his former mistress.

"Did I not tell you I was getting married and no longer required your services? Did I not make a generous settlement and encourage you to find another protector? What my wife did may be childish, but that doesn't change her directive for you to leave. It appears she and I agree on one thing."

When Mrs Everton stormed from the room, escorted by Barrington, Phillip looked at Lawrence, and his chuckles increased. His friend was sitting at his place at the table, his face bearing a bemused expression.

"When did I lose my staff to Charlotte?"

"When you sent her here for four months by herself to complete a herculean task."

Barrington returned to the room and placed the vase of flowers on the sideboard in their original position.

"I do so enjoy a floral arrangement, don't you?" Charlotte aimed her question at Phillip. Her innocent comment brought forth more chuckles.

Lawrence glared at the pair and pushed his chair away from the table. "I am done with this stupidity. Phillip, come and find me when you finish laughing like a fool."

Charlotte watched her husband stalk out of the room.

"The earl doesn't appear happy with my management of his mistress's presence here."

"He isn't happy that you doused her with water, but in his defence, he didn't invite her. When he chose to marry, he ended his relationship with Deslie. She must have taken it upon herself to come here uninvited. You did him a favour getting rid of her, although I don't think he will thank you."

"No, you're right there. The earl hasn't spoken a civil word to me. You know, don't you, I had nothing to do with a plan to fool him? If I had a hint of what my father intended, I would have refused to come."

"Lawrence can try to convince himself that you had a hand in the deception, but even he isn't blind enough that he can't see the truth."

"Is he too proud to admit he falsely accused me? The tenants, the staff and I have worked like skivvies to ready this place for his snooty lordship, and he intends to have the marriage annulled and bring my sister here to enjoy the fruits of my hard work. How fair is that? Has he even realised that this place was a dump when I arrived? He hasn't looked long enough to realise he has a beautiful home with productive tenants and lovely gardens. If he throws me out, I have nowhere to go. My father told me to make this work because I wasn't welcome at home. Where do I go? Do I go to the poorhouse or try to get a job as a servant at some other estate?"

Charlotte wept, and Phillip clenched his fists, wishing that Lawrence were here so he could punch him in the nose. Charlotte was in a difficult position and left at the mercy of a man who felt they had made him look a fool, and it didn't speak well of her prospects. Charlotte excused herself and cloistered herself in her bedroom, and when her weeping ceased, she sat on her bed and gazed around the room. This bedroom, which she had decorated to her tastes, was to become a room for her sister. The man Emma married would consummate their marriage in her bed, and she would give birth to her children there.

As Lawrence's bride, Emma would have been responsible for repairing the estate for her husband, and the task would have been beyond her. Charlotte was sure that Emma would have taken one look at the dilapidated manor and demanded to return to her father's house. Lawrence had made a better deal: marrying her. After her hard work, he intended to thank her by casting her out.

"Stop," Charlotte told herself. Nothing would be gained from hiding in the bedroom and letting the insufferable man think he had her beaten. If Lawrence ended the marriage, his life in this house would be a trial. He would need to hire a new steward, and his tenants would be uncooperative after his years of neglect. Lord Lawrence Clayhurst could choose to annul their wedding vows at his peril. Whatever satisfaction he got from thwarting her Father's devious plan would be dulled by years of living with tenants who hated him.

Chapter Eighteen

CHARLOTTE PUSHED LAWRENCE'S hateful words aside and settled in at her desk. Today, she needed to tally the estate costs and give Phillip the monthly figures. Charlotte opened the ledger book and dated a page for this week. Since she had taken over the accounts, she and Mrs Hatton tallied the weekly household spending. Neat columns of figures marched across the page as Charlotte prepared to enter last week's expenditure. The cost of running the estate had declined once the restoration had finished. The number of workers required to maintain the house and grounds was less than needed to bring the property into prime condition, so they saved on costs.

When the door opened, Charlotte looked up as her husband entered the room. She watched his eyes sweep over her and the desk's surface where she sat.

"What the devil are you doing? Did your father set you up to spy on my affairs? Do you have to report back to him on what you discover? Get out of my office, woman, and don't let me catch you in here again."

Charlotte rose, and a blush stained her cheeks. She put her hands on her hips and glared at her tormentor.

"I doubt you have been inside this room in the last six years, so calling it your office is rich. My father is a hateful, lying gambler, and I would never lower myself to do his bidding. It seems you share the malicious and dishonest characteristics with my father. I had hoped that my husband would treat me with respect. Regardless of my improvements to this place, you cannot manage thankfulness or respect. You proclaimed that your bride should repair and prepare your neglected estate for your arrival. I have complied with your mandate, whereas my sister was unable to do so. Do you believe the snobbish Emma would converse with your servants or get her hands dirty, as I have? The woman you chose would have fled the moment she saw this place, as derelict as it was. Have you looked around? Do you know what the property looked like when Molly and I arrived? I have worked as hard as the hired help, and all you can do is cast aspersions on my character. Your insults and abuse make me regret fixing the mess your years of neglect caused the estate. Well, damn you, my Lord."

Charlotte tilted her head up and walked from the room. She closed the door behind her and steadied herself on the wall. Her knees felt like jelly, and her hands shook. Every time she encountered the earl, he tore strips off her. She thought an annulment couldn't come soon enough. The problem with that solution was that she no longer had a home to return to, and with her reputation ruined, she could neither marry nor find decent employment.

As she walked up the stairs, she wondered what she should do. Phillip stepped towards her; his eyebrows arched in question.

"You look unhappier than you did this morning. Has something happened?"

"Yes, my esteemed husband found me doing the accounts and accused me of spying on his finances so I could tell my father. He might stop finding fault if he sat and listened to what I've done on the estate. I can do nothing right. He does not understand how hard the people and I worked, and he keeps looking for excuses to justify himself for not making sure his wife was the right woman."

"I'll speak with him now and see if he can act more reasonably."

"Good luck with that. I'm going for a ride. Margot in the village is with child, and she has been ill. I'll visit her for a while and then return through the fields. I'll see you later."

Phillip watched as Charlotte walked to her room. His heart ached for her. After four months of working as hard as the servants, Lawrence hadn't even commented on the excellent condition of the estate. Every time he spoke to her, he scolded her for an imagined slight. He knew Lawrence was not the only one duped by Whitely; Charlotte was, too. Her situation was ruinous. Lawrence had the moral right to have the marriage annulled, but it was Charlotte who would wear the shame of the failed marriage. And from what she said, when Lawrence had the marriage annulled, it wouldn't only ruin her reputation, but she would be homeless because her father refused to allow her to return to his home.

With a sigh, Phillip pushed the door of the office open. Lawrence looked up as his friend entered the room.

"Who has been doing the books? One set of books makes no sense, and the others start after our marriage. I'll have words with that woman if she hired a new steward."

"My friend, you need more information on what has happened over the last four months. Instead of jumping to conclusions, you should see for yourself what Charlotte has achieved. Your steward was robbing you, and the books that make no sense are his attempt at bookkeeping. When Charlotte fired the steward, we reclaimed bags of money he had hoarded instead of using them to buy seed. In conjunction with a long-time tenant, Charlotte has served as the steward and handled the books. Once I finish telling you what has happened, I suggest we ride around the estate so you can talk to your tenants and workers. I think the progress Charlotte has made will surprise you. Have you given a moment's thought to how the manor house looked when Charlotte arrived? Now, the place is clean and restored, and the gardens are a picture, rather than the jungle they were when she came. You need to speak with the tenants if you are unaware of the improvements to your home."

As Lawrence and Phillip rode towards the steward's home, guilt assailed Lawrence. Had he been unfair to Charlotte, considering the vast improvement she had made to his home in the four months he was in America? Lawrence was amazed when they arrived to visit Thomas, the man his wife had hired as the steward. How could she hire a crofter who knew nothing about ledgers? Lawrence dismounted his temper on a tight hold. Thomas greeted Phillip with familiarity, then Lawrence with deference.

"My wife appointed you as the steward after she fired the previous man. What qualifications do you have? Now that I am home, I will decide who to hire and who not to hire. And from what I can see, you have none of the traits I require from a steward."

Thomas regarded Lawrence with a furrowed brow.

"Lord Clayhurst, your wife did not hire me as the steward; we share the job. She doesn't have the time to oversee the planting, and I lack the book knowledge, so we share the duties. And begging your pardon, my lord, you're right. I don't possess any of the traits that the steward you hired possesses. He was a lying, cheating scumbag who nearly sent the estate broke. The tenants have spent years struggling to make a living because he took your money for the crop seed and didn't spend it as he was supposed to. We all thank the lord for your wife, and you should be proud of how she pulled this struggling estate from the brink of ruin."

Lawrence was unsure how to respond to a man who strongly supported his wife, and when he explained the arrangement for the steward's duties, it made sense to utilise the old-timer's knowledge. He mumbled about keeping up the excellent work and vaulted back onto his horse.

His wife, the woman he didn't want, had worked miracles with the estate. Lawrence and Phillip visited the tenants, and the praise for his wife was fulsome. No one spoke negatively. Lawrence discovered that she transported the workers to and from work, and that they had lunch. His head spun with the improvements and changes that Charlotte had made. She and Henry disposed of the extra horses, and the stables were immaculate under Henry's supervision. Even the gardens looked as though they had never been a mess of weeds and thistles, and the fountain on the lawns was white, and the water sparkled as it spewed from the upturned urn of the angel.

Lawrence owed her for restoring his property, but when she entered the room, his emotions became entangled, and his self-control deserted him. He didn't have an attraction to her, and he still intended to finish the marriage, but it impressed him to see how she had taken to her task of restoring his property. When the staff and servants loved her, why did she bring out the worst in him? It looked as though he might have to apologise to her for the unjustified criticisms. Apologies were not something he made a habit of, but he would need to make amends.

Lawrence wanted to apologise over the evening meal, but Charlotte thwarted his plans when she didn't arrive.

"Barrington, where is my wife?"

"My lord, Lady Charlotte, was unwell and ate on a tray in her room."

"Could you not have told me this before the meal?"

Barrington gave him a blank look.

"Sorry, my lord; nobody thought you would care."

The earl's face darkened, and his cheeks flushed. An explosion of temper was imminent, and Barrington straightened his posture and tilted his chin, expecting to bear the brunt of the rage. Lawrence stood and pointed a finger at the butler.

"Get out and take the servers with you."

Lawrence rubbed a hand across his face and sank into the chair once the staff left the room.

"Why is it every time that woman is around, she makes me lose my temper? Damnation, she's not even here, and she makes me angry."

"Only you can answer that question, but did you give anyone the impression that you cared about Charlotte's whereabouts? Barrington said what all the staff think. You blame the woman they love and respect for a crime they doubt she carried out. If you intend to get rid of her, you must travel to London and address the issue. But before you make a rash decision, have you considered what the annulment will do to Charlotte?"

"What do you mean?"

"You annul the marriage, and it will ruin Charlotte's reputation. No one will believe you haven't consummated the marriage, so that she will bear the shame of the dissolution. No decent man would offer for her, and as her Father told her not to return home if the marriage didn't work, she would be homeless. So, after you restore your pride, you will be left with a shrew for a wife and a ruined maiden."

"I have to do this. If others heard of the scam, I would be the laughing stock of the ton."

"Better to be laughed at than to live with a shrew and have the ruination of a young woman on your conscience. And perhaps before you dismiss Charlotte, you might like to offer her your thanks for what she has achieved. Not once have you thanked her for her work. This place was in ruins, the tenants were starving, and the fields were empty. The task you gave her was monumental, and she rolled up her sleeves and got to work. A lesser person would have taken one look at the place and bolted in the other direction. Whatever beef you have with Whitely is not Charlotte's fault. Be the bigger man, Lawrence and thank her."

Lawrence had the decency to look guilty because Phillip was correct in all that he said.

Chapter Nineteen

CHARLOTTE SAT ON THE edge of the bed. Molly had helped her disrobe, and now she sat dressed in the only chemise she owned. She rose and walked to the window. The night was bleak; no moon would light a traveller's way. She shivered as a breeze trickled through the poorly fitted window. How long before she was adrift, like the travellers on a moonless night? When the earl went to London to collect her sister and dissolve their marriage, he intended to cast her aside as though she were yesterday's garbage. Her future looked bleak. She had little to look forward to; the prospect of living in the workhouse loomed large.

She had nothing to gain from these dark thoughts, but her brain was too busy to fall asleep. Charlotte decided to visit the library downstairs, hoping to find a book to distract her. The house was still; the residents were abed for the night. If she had another option, she would not choose to walk through the house in her chemise, but the prospect of trying to dress without Molly's aid was daunting. Surely, no one else was wondering this late at night?

Charlotte opened the door to her room and peered along the corridor. There was not a soul in sight. The earl's adjoining room was dark and silent. No one would see her if she visited the library. She closed the door behind her and held the candle high as she tiptoed along the hallway. As she passed Lawrence's door, she held her breath, loath to give away her presence. A few treads on the stairs creaked, but Charlotte had been at the house long enough to avoid them.

With a sigh of relief, she pushed open the library door. The room was dark except for the glow emanating from her candle. She placed the candle in the sconce and moved towards the shelf. As she reached out for a book, the door opened. A candle preceded a person into the room. When someone placed the second candle in the sconce, Charlotte recognised her companion; it was the Earl. She groaned. The Earl made her heart race in fear and anger. She wanted nothing to do with him. When she raised her eyes, she stepped back at the fury etched on his face.

"What the hell are you doing skulking around the house in your chemise?" he hissed.

"Uh, I'm having trouble falling asleep and hoped reading might make me drowsy."

"You must think I'm a fool. I don't, for a minute, believe you were looking for a book while dressed in your chemise. Where is the book? Which footman did you agree to meet?"

Charlotte rocked back on her heels as though he had slapped her. Her heart raced, and the colour drained from her face. With gritted teeth, she stepped forward, and the crack of her hand on his face echoed in the silent room.

"You disgust me. Just because you have a mistress doesn't mean we are all as morally corrupt as you. I took marriage vows in good faith, and even though you can't bring yourself to touch me, it doesn't mean I will be whoring myself around your estate. Move aside so I can leave."

"What will you do if I refuse to move? Scream? The entire household will see you and me alone in the library with you in your chemise. That should cause talk."

A disbelieving laugh escaped Charlotte's lips.

"They might think you intended to fulfil your marital obligations."

Before she could step away from Lawrence, he reached out and hooked his hand behind her neck. He pulled her towards him, and her heart fluttered. What were his intentions? Was he going to hurt her? Her breasts pressed against his chest, and when he lowered his lips to hers, Charlotte felt like she might swoon. She froze, not sure what to do. No one had ever kissed her in this way. She had endured the occasional kiss on the cheek, but this kiss was very different. Lawrence nipped and licked and sucked her lips. The feel of his warm, soft mouth against hers was heavenly.

"Open your mouth," he instructed.

Charlotte fisted her hands in his shirt, and a quiet groan escaped her mouth. Lost in a daze, it took a moment for the command to filter through her brain. Opening her mouth, she found the earl's lips encasing hers, and then his tongue flicked against hers and began a slow exploration of her mouth's warm, wet depth.

Lawrence's hands clasped her waist, but he fisted his hands in her hair as the kiss continued. His fingers in her thick, silky locks held her in place as he continued exploring. Lawrence's body heat and scent invaded Charlotte's. A slow burn assaulted her. She squirmed closer to Lawrence, seeking something she couldn't name.

Damnation, what was he thinking, kissing her? The infuriating woman unsettled him, and his anger flared. He needed to put distance between them lest he lose his head completely. When the earl stepped back, Charlotte moaned and swayed on her feet. He watched her face and recognised that the unfocused, sleepy eyes were filled with desire. His bookish little wife had a passionate nature; who would have thought it? When Charlotte pressed her body against his and her breasts pushed against his chest, he understood Phillip's comment about her feminine shape. Charlotte was standing where he had left her with a lost look. If Lawrence didn't send her away, he knew he might consummate the marriage here in the library. He chuckled and sneered at the woman standing in front of him.

"Get out of here. Go back to bed, and don't wander the halls again."

Charlotte drew herself up and moved past him at the terse tone of the earl's voice. By the time she reached the hall, she was almost running. She would not be able to sleep now if she had not been able to sleep before her encounter with her husband.

85

Chapter Twenty

EARLY THE FOLLOWING day, Charlotte dithered, deciding whether to go to breakfast or eat in her room. Could she face the earl after what had transpired between them the previous night? With her fingers pressed against her temple, Charlotte tried to focus on her dilemma. It would be best if you showed courage, she told herself. During the day, she would see him; she might as well do it now.

When she walked into the breakfast room, Barrington greeted her with a smile and pulled out a chair for her. Phillip sat to her right, and the Earl sat at the head of the table. Charlotte smiled at Phillip, greeted him, and gave her husband a brisk good morning. Phillip and Charlotte exchanged small talk, which startled her when the earl barked a question.

"You don't appear to have slept well, Charlotte. Did you spend too much time wandering around the house last night?"

Phillip's confusion at the change of the topic was apparent, but Charlotte blushed at the reference to the previous night's activities.

"Thank you, my lord; I slept well."

"Should I take credit for your sound sleep?"

Charlotte choked on the mouthful of tea she had just taken.

"Barrington, could you give us privacy? The servers can also leave. I'll call you if we need anything."

Once the staff had left, Charlotte faced the Earl.

"If you have something to say, for god's sake, spit it out. I want to eat my breakfast, not wait in suspense for you to drop more hints."

The Earl laughed, although there was nothing joyous or happy about it to Charlotte's ears.

"I thought I might ask Phillip what he thinks of the lady of the house walking around in her chemise. I suspect a midnight tryst with a footman, although my wife vehemently denies that; the evidence points to a rendezvous."

Phillip looked up from his plate. "What?"

Lawrence linked his hands together and placed them on his head as he leaned back in his chair. The stance was cocky and smug, and Charlotte was sure the conversation would disintegrate into accusations. She shook her head and glanced at Phillip.

"Last night, I couldn't sleep. I visited the library to get a book. The house was silent, and instead of disturbing everyone by calling for Molly to help me dress, I went downstairs in my chemise. I didn't expect to meet anyone."

Phillip groaned. "Your plan didn't go as planned, and Lawrence was wandering around the house. Why didn't you put on a pelisse?"

"Why, indeed?"

A look passed between the two, and Phillip said, "Oh."

"It appears Phillip has information that I don't. Why didn't you wear a pelisse or a shawl?"

Charlotte stood, glaring at this man who was supposed to be her husband.

"See this ugly dress? It is one of the two dresses I own. I'm sure Phillip can fill you in later."

"Fancy dresses won't make any difference. Someone who responds to advances as wantonly as you did won't have to worry about proper clothes."

Charlotte's face flamed. "Excuse me if I don't know how to respond to kisses. I thought it should be enjoyable for the woman and the man. Why am I to blame? You kissed me, not the other way around. I'm so glad that you intend to end our marriage. Your wealth will help my sister close her eyes and lie still while you throw up her skirt and force yourself on her."

As she pushed her chair back, Phillip cursed.

"Damn it, man."

She heard no more as she raced for the door, where she nearly collided with Barrington.

"Is everything all right, milady?"

"Yes. Will you please find Molly, and if she has finished eating, I need her help to tie my hair back; I intend to go riding."

Charlotte went to her room, grateful for the diversion that riding through the estate would afford her. With his wife's swift exit, the silence in the room was overwhelming. Phillip looked at Lawrence with amazement.

"You kissed her last night and ridiculed her this morning for her response? What the hell is wrong with you, Lawrence? Do you deliberately provoke her, or are you so dull-witted that you accidentally offend her?"

"Well, you won't have to worry about my treatment of my little wife after today; I intend to head to the city as soon as I finish eating."

"Will you tell Charlotte where you are going?"

"If I see her, I will."

As Henry and the grooms assisted Charlotte to mount, Lawrence and Phillip left the house. They both carried a small bag. Once Charlotte mounted her horse, Ben, the accompanying groom for the day, vaulted into the saddle. Before they could move their horses away, the Earl approached Charlotte.

"Phillip and I are travelling to London. When I return, I will have your sister with me. Make sure the staff prepare the house for their future mistress."

Charlotte wheeled around on her horse and kicked the startled beast into a canter. A peal of laughter behind her made her grit her teeth. Never had Charlotte felt so ashamed. Her husband was flaunting his intentions to end their marriage in front of the staff. Even though servants knew everything that happened inside a house, he could be discreet for her sake. Charlotte rode through the fallow paddocks towards the estate's bushland with the groom beside her. She kept her mount at a steady canter and tried to burn off her shame and frustration.

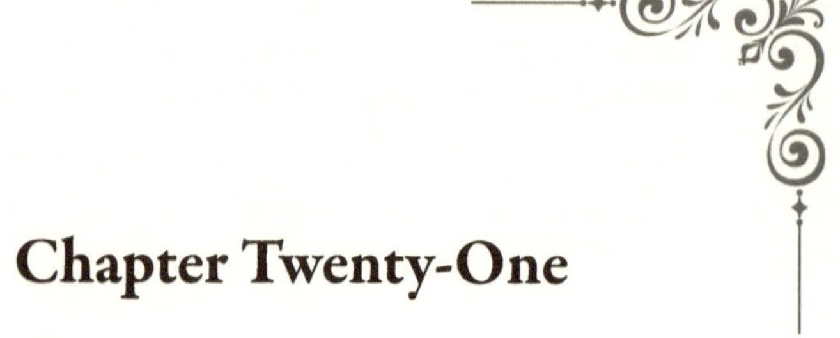

Chapter Twenty-One

THE EARL AND PHILLIP started their trip at a fast clip, and though the journey took three days in a carriage, travelling light and using horses, they could complete the ride in two. The trick to managing the horses was to vary their maintained speeds and rest when necessary. Once the horses were walking in sync, Phillip asked the question that had nagged at him since breakfast this morning.

"Why did you call Charlotte wanton? Why did you tell her you prefer a woman to lie still and close her eyes when she is in your bed? No man would choose a log of wood if he could have a warm, willing bedmate."

Lawrence rubbed the back of his neck and sighed.

"I can't control my mouth when she is close to me. Her father fooled me, and I can't be sure she wasn't in on the deception. The hoax she and her father pulled stirs my anger when she is present, and I vent my frustration on her."

"Traipsing after her sister is a foolish move, but at least it will remove the doubt regarding Charlotte's honesty. Why saddle yourself with a woman concerned with your financial state, not your well-being?"

"It's the principle of the matter."

"Being right will not console you in a few years when you sit across the table from her scowling face. She will make you miserable. When you meet the sister, if your pride doesn't blind you, you will see what a nasty, mean trollop she is. Had Whitely sent her when you married, she would have bolted for her Father's house and demanded an annulment. But faced with an estate in disrepair, Charlotte rolled up her sleeves and set about following your instructions. If a well-to-do man sees Charlotte's worth, the staff will follow her wherever she lives."

The journey continued in silence, each man plagued by their thoughts. Lawrence broke the silence.

"What do you know about the ugly dress?"

As Phillip related the story of Charlotte's poor treatment by her father and the saga of the empty trunk, Lawrence listened, and his anger burned.

"The bloody man used the money to outfit Emma when my instructions were explicit. I will take the man to task when we meet him."

"Well, it doesn't matter now. Your wife will have beautiful clothes, and Charlotte will have her ugly dress. Did you know that the dress is a step up from what she wore at Whiteley's estate? The cursed man would give her no money for clothes, so that she would raid the poor box at the church. Emma could have shared her dress money with Charlotte, but refused to do so, and while Charlotte worked as the steward and the housekeeper, her sister entertained the ladies of the ton."

Lawrence couldn't believe what he was hearing. What kind of father used his daughter as the housekeeper and the steward and refused her money for decent clothes?

When they reached their accommodations in London, Lawrence wanted to confront Arthur Whitely that day. Phillip recommended a plan of action to prevent Whitely from turning the tables on them. The earl sent a message requesting a meeting the following day. When a favourable response arrived, the men spent the night planning how to approach the man. Even though Lawrence was angry about the ruse, he realised that dropping Charlotte back into her father's house without a protection plan was wrong. Even though he had never thanked

Charlotte for her Herculean effort to bring the estate back from ruin, he appreciated her efforts and couldn't, in good conscience, dump her at her father's house without repaying his debt.

Early the next day, Lawrence and Phillip approached the house. The shabbiness encroached on the building and its surrounding gardens.

"This place will collapse soon if the fool doesn't improve his management."

A few minutes after Lawrence rapped on the aging wooden door, the old retainer opened the door.

"Lord Clayhurst, the baron, is expecting you."

The servant led the way along hallways furnished with tattered runners. The state of the house appalled Phillip. Lawrence raised an eyebrow and said to the butler, "You miss Charlotte's organisation, do you?"

"Yes, milord, she kept the place running, and without her, the entire home is collapsing around us. Most staff haven't received their pay, and the creditors are threatening to evict the family." Lawrence watched as the man wrung his hands.

A scowl appeared on Lawrence's face. How could the man have so little regard for the family and his servants?

Williams tapped on the door and ushered Phillip and Lawrence into the room. Whitely rose to greet the men, a malicious smile on his face.

"How goes married life, Lord Clayhurst?"

"You played a trick on me, but I always get what I want. I want the other sister, and if you comply, I will send Charlotte back to you to organise your financial problems."

"Don't bother sending that baggage back to me. Charlotte is not my offspring, and I'll not have her here."

"What do you expect me to do with her? This fiasco was of your making. Did the chit know that you sent her instead of her sister?"

"No. Charlotte would have refused to go if she had known I was pulling a ruse on you. Why are you whining? I did you a favour. Charlotte may be a thorn in my side, but I bet she dragged your abandoned estate into a profitable enterprise. Unlike Charlotte, Emma is a lady, and the task you wanted her to complete would be beyond her. Charlotte was always up to her elbows in crops, menus, and tenants' babies. Emma does not lower herself to complete tasks that aren't befitting of a lady. If you want a workhorse, you'd best keep Charlotte."

"From the state of the house, it seems that you need Charlotte to return."

"If she arrives at the house, I'll call the authorities and have them remove her to the workhouse."

Phillip remained quiet, but his facial expressions told the story of his contempt for Arthur Whitely.

Lawrence paced across the room. "When I paid your gambling debts, I stupidly supposed that without those debts weighing you down, you could move forward and be able to pay your staff and feed your family. It seems you've just been sitting in this room, drinking brandy. The house is falling apart, yet the woman who can fix this mess is someone you refuse to have in your home. It makes no sense. I have a business proposition for you, but I would appreciate it if your wife and daughter could also be present. When can we talk to the three of you?"

"My wife never socialises."

"I don't blame the woman. Who would want to be in the company of a man who questions her honesty? If you want your financial problems sorted, encourage her and your daughter to join us."

Chapter Twenty-Two

FACED WITH THE PROSPECT of Charlotte being left homeless, Lawrence had to find a solution. Phillip and Lawrence discussed an idea, and although not foolproof, it might give Charlotte some security when she returned home. At the approved visiting hour, the men knocked on the door of the home of Arthur Whitely. Williams once again answered the door, and this time, he escorted them to the drawing room. The room was as shabby as the rest of the house.

When Whitely rose, he introduced his daughter and wife to the visitors. Lawrence was interested in both women. The petite blonde in the faultless turnout was the woman he asked to marry him to pay Whitely's debts. Whitely was right; the younger sister was a lady, and with her attire and superior attitude, Lawrence felt a moment of concern. Was he making a mistake in insisting on marrying this woman? Lawrence pushed his doubts aside; he had requested his sister, and Whitely had tricked him. He intended to get what was rightfully his. The second woman was tall, and her facial structure reminded him of Charlotte. Her brown hair would have been lighter than Charlotte's in her youth. But as she aged, streaks of grey began to show among the deep brown.

A maid arrived with a tea tray, and Emma poured. They exchanged no pleasantries because Lawrence wanted to resolve this situation quickly.

"Lady Whitely, you know that your husband and I made a deal regarding paying his debts? Your husband chose the opportunity to trick me, and I am here to clear up the problem caused by the deception."

Lady Whitely looked at her husband.

"What does this have to do with Emma and me? As gentlemen, can't you work out the business without troubling the womenfolk of the house?"

"Ah, but it has everything to do with you, ladies. Your husband and I agreed that the sister I would wed was Emma, not Charlotte."

Both women gasped, and Emma paled.

"As the wedding was by proxy, I didn't see my bride until my return from the Americas. I wish to discuss business with you, not your husband, because I know he isn't trustworthy. The clothes you are wearing, Miss Emma, were for my wife. As your father sent your sister instead of you, the clothes should have been hers."

Emma blushed and fluttered her eyelashes at the two men.

"It was for the best, my lord. Charlotte isn't interested in quality clothes. It would be a waste to outfit her."

Phillip, who had said very little up to this point, laughed. The sound in the silent room was both explosive and rude. He looked directly at Emma, refusing to apologise for his rudeness.

"Miss Emma, fluttering your eyelashes while disparaging your sister does not change the facts. Your nasty, spiteful comments about your sister at the wedding reflect poorly on you, not on her. They speak to the type of character you are. It confounds me why Lawrence wants you as a wife when he already has a perfect candidate. But I guess to each their own. What kind of sister are you, parading around town in stylish clothes while Charlotte wore rags? I know she sourced her clothes from the poor box at the church while you paraded around in new dresses. Instead of clothes befitting her station, she arrived with nothing, as your father emptied her trunk before he loaded it onto the coach. You, Whitely, disowned Charlotte, proving what a foolish decision you made. When I look at Lady Elizabeth, I can see Charlotte in her. Charlotte is a little taller, but Lady Elizabeth's hair in her youth would have been the same colour and texture as Charlotte's. The shape of their faces is identical, and their eyes are the same colour."

Lady Whitely leant across the small table and patted Phillip on the hand.

"Thank you, Mr Hilderbrand. I have been unable to prove that Charlotte was Arthur's daughter for years. It pleases me that you can see the likeness."

Arthur Whitely growled. "What is this business you want to discuss?"

Lawrence stood and walked to the window.

"Despite your unreasonable dislike of Charlotte, she has kept the household going. You need to rid yourself of this property, and I will exchange it for a townhouse. Lady Whitely, you must take charge of the household expenses and hold the purse strings."

Baron Whitely jumped to his feet. "This is outrageous! What man would turn over the financial matters to his wife?"

"You will; otherwise, I will leave you in this run-down house. I will offer your wife, servants, and daughter a home without you. The choice is yours, Whitely."

Whitely's face was a brilliant red, and his body vibrated angrily. Lawrence moved so he was standing in the baron's line of sight. "There are two other conditions. First, the woman I chose as my bride will become my wife as soon as I have annulled my marriage to Charlotte. My second condition is that when Emma moves into my estate, Charlotte will return to your new home as a full household member."

The silence in the room was profound. The expressions on the faces of the baron's family ranged from thoughtful, excited and angry. Lawrence remained quiet, allowing the family to break the silence first.

Emma was the first person to speak. "Why should I become your wife?"

"Your father made a bargain, and your marriage to me was part of that deal. You have the clothes for my wife, and I can offer you a comfortable lifestyle. We will rub along well enough together; I don't have time to woo a woman only for her to run me around."

Lady Elizabeth cleared her throat.

"Excuse me, Lord Clayhurst, there is one problem nobody seems keen to discuss. Between you and my husband, you have ruined my daughter. After living at your estate for over four months, her ruined reputation will mean she spends the rest of her life as a spinster. Can you not reconsider and settle for Charlotte as your wife? She has a caring heart and is kind to those she encounters. You could do a lot worse than to remain married to Charlotte."

Lawrence stood and looked down at Charlotte's mother.

"I understand your concern, Lady Elizabeth, but your husband and I had a deal, and I am here to ensure he rectifies matters and keeps up his end of the bargain. After addressing the issues your husband has caused, we can explore potential suitors for Charlotte. A large financial incentive should help men with empty pockets to overlook her ruined reputation."

"So Emma marries an Earl, and you men sell Charlotte to a wastrel with no money. Your sense of justice astounds me, Lord Clayhurst."

After an awkward silence, the business agreement details kept the room occupants busy for a few more hours. When they dealt with the problems the baron persisted in raising, Lawrence said, "It's agreed then? Lady Whitely, Phillip, will collect you to look at the townhouse in the morning. Baron, you may go if you wish, but the decision is your wife's. Emma, I will collect you, and we will ride through the park."

Lawrence's drive in the park was everything he wanted to avoid when he chose his bride by forcing Whitley into surrendering his daughter. Society's most prestigious dowagers and matrons called to Lawrence and eyed his companion with beady eyes. Despite their polite conversation, the news that Lawrence accompanied his sister-in-law would sweep the ton faster than a chill wind.

The sticky beaks would have been bearable had the conversation with his intended been interesting, but the discussion concerned her and her social events. She never asked about her sister's welfare, and her comments about the revitalised estate centred on how much she looked forward to decorating a house she had never seen. Her questions about his preference for the new fad of Egyptian-inspired decorations made him frown. Charlotte hadn't redecorated any rooms he had seen, although she may have changed her bedchamber when he thought about it. Why would the redecoration be high on Emma's list?

As she prattled on, Lawrence lost patience and instructed the driver to return to the house. For the first time since his anger forced him to drive to town to claim what was rightfully his, Lawrence wondered if he was doing the right thing. Should he swallow his pride, accept Charlotte as his bride, and leave this self-centred debutant alone? Lawrence knew what Phillip would tell him, but the thought of Whiteley's smirk firmed his resolve. He would have the bride he chose, and the other one could return to her home.

Chapter Twenty-Three

LAWRENCE AND PHILLIP had left a week ago, and there was no telling how long the trip would take. Charlotte muddled through the next few days. She found it difficult to concentrate on the jobs she regularly completed without trouble.

As she dressed the following day in her ugly, all-purpose dress, Charlotte could see herself dressed in this outfit for the rest of her life. She slumped onto the bed and still sat there when Molly entered the room.

"Molly, what has my life become? I have a husband who intends to get rid of me. All my hard work restoring the estate will be for naught because my sister will benefit from our efforts, and I have only this ugly gown to show for the last five months of my life. When Lawrence evicts me, I have nowhere to go and nothing but this horrid dress to wear.

Molly hated to see her mistress defeated. The earl's constant criticism and anger chipped away at her determination and the spark of her personality. Even with the man gone, the pall of gloom he triggered hung on like fog on a cloudy day. Molly glanced at her mistress; the ugly dress hung like a sack. When an idea formed in her mind, a slow smile spread across Molly's face, and she laughed out loud.

Charlotte looked over at her maid, her gloom interrupted by surprise as she heard Molly's laughter.

"I'm glad my misery causes you joy," she snapped.

"No, milady, not your misery; your dress causes me to laugh. Why are you wearing that ugly dress when your husband is wealthy? Should we not go to a dressmaker so you can dress appropriately for your position? He is still your husband until the earl ends your marriage; you should dress accordingly."

The possibilities crowded Charlotte's mind. Fashionable clothes to take away from this marriage would at least leave her with something to show for this fiasco. Her spirits lifted, and she smiled at Molly.

"Brilliant idea, Molly. Let's see if either Mrs Hatten or Barrington knows of a dressmaker in a town nearby. We need a brief holiday."

Charlotte and Molly entered the kitchen. Mrs Hatten poured the tea as Charlotte and Molly took their seats. With the tea dispensed to those at the table, Charlotte spoke.

"I need help, and as you two have been my co-conspirators in restoring the estate, I hoped you might offer advice."

Barrington and Mrs Hatton nodded their heads in agreement.

"We will do whatever we can to help, Lady Charlotte."

Charlotte explained her need to find a dressmaker capable of creating an extensive wardrobe. Mrs Hatton slapped her knee and let out an unladylike chortle. Barrington chuckled as he nodded his head. The approval of the two stalwarts warmed Charlotte's heart and reaffirmed her desire to come out of this marriage with something for her efforts.

The carriage rocked as the horses crested the rise. From their vantage point at the windows, Molly and Charlotte could see the town of Windemere spread out before them. Barrington had been true to his word; this town appeared to be a bustling business centre. Charlotte hoped that the seamstress, recommended by the mistress of one of Barrington's cousins, was ready to take orders and deliver garments over the following week.

After navigating the busy streets, Henry halted outside the porch of a large, elaborate building. The hotel was to be home while Charlotte waited for her new clothes. After spending the night in a rooming house, the stable lads accompanying Charlotte returned to the estate.

After the seamstress finished the clothes that Charlotte needed, the outriders would return to Windemere to accompany the carriage as it travelled back to the Clayhurst estate.

Charlotte was so excited to have free rein over what she purchased that the following days passed in a blur. The women endlessly scrutinised rolls of material and viewed pictures of the latest fashions, aware that this was their only chance to refurbish Charlotte's wardrobe. When Lawrence arrived with her sister in tow, Charlotte knew her sister would pressure Lawrence to withhold funds from her, and that she would once again be wearing the cast-offs of others. Once the women had chosen the fabric and the seamstress had taken Charlotte's measurements, they left the shop to visit a bootmaker and a milliner.

"I hope Phillip pays these bills, or we will both be in the poorhouse quickly."

"He will pay for them. I suspect that Mr Phillip has developed a soft spot for you."

Charlotte blushed, all the while denying Molly's claim. Molly grinned at her mistress and shook her head to show she didn't believe her assertions.

At the end of the first week, Charlotte received half the clothes she had ordered: shoes, boots, slippers, and hats. Molly watched Charlotte's excitement, her face wreathed in smiles. Their shopping expedition would be a happy memory that Charlotte would remember, regardless of what happened in her marriage. Her achievement in restoring Lawrence's estate deserved recognition and celebration, but if her husband didn't give her credit, she would celebrate with Molly for company.

"This is better than any Christmas I have ever had. I want to run around singing or dancing. How good is this? Thank you for suggesting a shopping spree. It has revived my spirits. What would you say if I let Henry know we will leave as soon as the outriders arrive? After we leave, the shopkeepers can send the clothes to the estate; I doubt any alterations will be needed. Mrs Weston took measurements of every part of me, and so far, the lovely dresses she sent over fit well."

Molly smiled.

"That is a good suggestion. We would hate to be absent when the master returns with your sister. I can't wait to see their faces when they see you dressed in your finery. Imagine your sister's shock when she realises how beautiful you are, and I think the master will regret his hasty actions."

"Your shopping suggestion was brilliant, but I will regret leaving the estate. We worked hard to restore it, but my sister won't be caring for the tenants or their families. She will bully the staff, and they feel like family to me. And she will hobnob in society, being as fake as those dowagers who pass judgments on people."

For a moment, Charlotte looked sad, but the excitement of the packages they had loaded in the carriage restored her good humour. The shocked looks on her husband's and her sister's faces when they saw her dressed in her finery gladdened her heart.

Chapter Twenty-Four

"WHY DOES THE RETURN journey always feel longer than the outward journey?" Charlotte asked Molly. While the journey was no longer Charlotte's anticipation of showing Mrs Hatton and Barrington, the purchases made the trip seem endless. They broke their journey with an overnight stop in a respectable inn and set out early the next day, hoping to reach Clayhurst Manor in the early afternoon. The women had filled the trunks they used on their initial trip to the Clayhurst estate with their purchases, and the garments that wouldn't fit into the compartments lined the seat opposite Charlotte, with many boxes stacked on the floor. Charlotte was eager to show her purchases to her co-conspirators. Ever the thoughtful one, she had purchased gifts for the staff.

Charlotte smiled as they passed through the fields, seeing the crops poking their heads up from the fertile soil. The village looked affluent, with repairs already completed to most of the dwellings, and whatever happened with her husband, Charlotte felt a sense of pride at what she had achieved.

The footmen had loaded the carriage with the trunks of clothes and accessories, along with Charlotte's clothes, and two bolts of material for the women of the town and tenant farms. They had suffered because of Lawrence's lack of interest in the estate after his father's death, and Charlotte believed in sharing his largesse with those folks. She gave her husband a moment's thought, then shrugged. Who cared what he thought? Soon enough, he would make her leave the estate, and she intended to leave a small legacy for the town's folk.

When the carriage stopped on the circular drive, Charlotte had to control the urge to leap out of the vehicle. The carriage door opened, and a beaming Barrington held out a hand to Charlotte and Molly.

"Lady Charlotte, we are excited to have you back. The load in the carriage suggests your shopping went well," he grinned.

"Barrington, Molly, and I had so much fun. I bought presents for everyone and also items for the townsfolk. I did so much enjoy spending his lordship's money!"

Mrs Hatton poked her head out the door.

"For goodness' sake, Barrington, let Lady Charlotte in the door instead of standing there talking."

"Mrs Hatton, it's nice to be home. Molly and I will have a pot of tea and then a bath. Barrington, could you organise the baths, please? The outriders can go home as soon as they put the carriage up, and Henry can join us for a drink or go home, whichever he prefers. Let the outriders and Henry know they can have tomorrow off after accompanying me on my trip."

Barrington left to do Charlotte's bidding, and Molly and Charlotte plopped on the chairs in the breakfast room. Mrs Hatton loaded the table with plates of hearty slabs of fruit cake, bread and cheese. Charlotte and Molly chatted to Mrs Hatton while Barrington organised the footmen to draw two baths. Mrs Hatton watched Charlotte's face, alive with enthusiasm as she talked about the clothes and other purchases. If spending the earl's money replaced the sad, hopeless look in her mistress's eye, she was all for it.

After Charlotte presented the staff with her gifts, she and Molly headed for the privacy of their rooms and the hot baths. Mrs Hatton shook her head.

"How is it, Barrington, that we all see the lovely woman that Lady Charlotte is, but his lordship prefers the other sister? Mr Hilderbrand said that one is all show and no substance. Mark my words; she will make our lives miserable as she tries to set herself up in the aristocracy's hierarchy that frequents this district."

"Why is his lordship so blind? If there were something we could do, I would. I fear the other one will be the mistress here, sooner rather than later."

Mrs Hatton sighed. "Men."

The following day, Charlotte visited the tenant farmers' wives. She called on the seamstress who had sewn her plain brown gowns and gifted her the two bolts of cloth. She handed out small trinkets to the ladies and sweets to the children.

"The cloth is for everyone to use, but a few women cannot sew, so if I leave it here, you might help them. I bought needles and spools of thread to use. Everyone looks as though they need fresh clothes. If you need more, just let me know, and I will arrange more supplies."

On the ride home, Charlotte and her groom, Ben, took a detour. The estate was under cultivation, but the riding paths were alongside the fields. The track she had taken weaved through a large copse of trees. Dressed in her new habit, Charlotte enjoyed the wind in her face, the horse's hooves beating a tattoo on the soft dirt. As she pulled her horse to a walk, the beauty of her surroundings and the compliant horse under her made her think that life couldn't get any better. She grinned at the groom as they rode alongside each other.

With a sigh, Charlotte turned the horse for home. She chatted with Ben as they returned across the tracks they had earlier cantered over. While a conversation between the mistress of the house and a groom was not standard, Charlotte refused to ride, ignoring the man who, for her safety, accompanied her. When they reached the stable, an agitated Henry met them. He held Charlotte's horse, and Ben lifted her from the saddle. Once on the ground, the cause of Henry's distress became obvious. The carriage horses stood in the walkway, their sides heaving, sweat running along their necks and flanks.

"What on earth happened to the horses? Did they bolt or something? They are a total mess."

Henry growled, the sound low and angry.

"Miss Emma was tired of sitting in the carriage, so the Earl told the driver to push the horses."

"So, my husband and sister are here."

"Yes, and the rider who came in to tell us of their imminent arrival informed us that the earl wanted the staff lined up out the front to meet their prospective mistress."

Charlotte's face flushed scarlet at this news. A lump formed in her throat, and she could not comment on Henry's report. With a loud sigh, Charlotte turned tail and walked towards the entrance to the house. Henry watched her go, his sorrow for this young woman evident in his eyes. Ben shook his head as he watched Charlotte walk towards the house. Having spent many hours accompanying her, Ben felt he knew Charlotte well. Her refusal to ride ahead of him warmed his heart, and their conversations as they rode were enjoyable and often enlightening.

"What the hell is wrong with his Lordship? He has Lady Charlotte as his wife and wants to reject her. Is the man mad?"

Henry shook his head. "I fear he might be Ben; I fear he might just be."

Chapter Twenty-Five

AS CHARLOTTE WALKED towards the front door, the enjoyment of her ride with Ben began to dim. How could Lawrence do this to her? The humiliation was almost worse than his scorn. Presenting the staff to Emma was a slap in the face, given her arrival had been without fanfare. Why had her sister agreed to the arrangement? Surely, some sisterly concern would cause Emma to refuse Lawrence's demands? Charlotte realised that Emma's refusal to share the money her father gave her was not because of her desire not to run foul of her father, but to exercise her superiority over her sister. The sisters had never been close, but Emma's willingness to assist the earl in ruining her was hurtful.

When Charlotte entered the house, she encountered many trunks lined up along the bottom of the stairwell. Servants ran back and forth, carrying armloads of clothes from one room to another.

"What is going on here?"

As Barrington bustled downstairs, the unperturbable butler was wringing his hands.

"My lady, his lordship, has instructed us to move you to one of the guest rooms and to place your sister in the room adjoining his."

Charlotte gasped at the news. "Stop what you are doing."

The servants, who had been scurrying around like ants moments ago, all stopped their activities and looked at her.

"You will cease your work until I return. Where is his lordship?"

"He and Miss Emma are in the drawing-room with Mr Phillip, my lady."

Charlotte strode towards the door. Barrington hustled to open the door for her. She noticed how close Lawrence and her sister sat as she entered the room. Phillip rose to greet her, and she smiled at him.

"Charlotte, how lovely to see you!"

"Phillip, I am always pleased to see you; you are the shining star in my marriage's mess. Did I ever tell you I often regret that you weren't the groom on my wedding day? I have unpleasant business I need to discuss with his lordship. If you wish to leave, now would be a great time."

"My dear wife, will you not greet your husband and sister? I'm sure you have nothing to say to me that is too harsh for Phillip's ears."

"Very well. I have no greeting for a faithless husband and a sister who participates in the ruination of her sibling. Are you and I still married, my lord?" she asked, her voice laced with sarcasm.

"For the moment, we are. I wanted Emma to be sure she felt happy here at my estate, so I delayed the annulment of our relationship."

Placing her hands on her hips, Charlotte stood over the earl, who had remained seated. "Are you so caught up in besting my father that you don't care who else you damage?"

"What are you on about, woman?"

"When you end this farce of a marriage, my reputation will be in shreds. I will never marry and have a family because no man will want me, but let's not worry about me. If you move her into your adjoining room, you will destroy Emma's reputation. Why do you imagine that placing a single woman, who is your sister-in-law, in the connecting bedroom is proper behaviour? Before you get a ring on her finger, the women of the surrounding county will ostracise her as soon as they hear of the bedroom arrangement."

Lawrence's face was an ugly shade of red, and he clenched his fists as he rose from the table.

"I will instruct the staff not to gossip about our arrangements."

Charlotte gave an unladylike snort. "Your staff hates you for what you are doing to me. They will take great delight in spreading the news of the unusual bedding arrangements in this house. There is no loyalty to a fickle, self-centred aristocrat. You can give them instructions, but you will not know whether they pay heed to your edict until the society matrons meet Emma."

Phillip joined the conversation.

"Lawrence, Charlotte speaks the truth. If you put your sister-in-law in an adjoining room, it will cause a scandal. Do you hate Charlotte so much that you choose to humiliate her in her own home?"

Lawrence glared at Phillip for a moment. He hated to be wrong, and while he could ignore Charlotte, it was harder to ignore the advice of his friend.

"Very well. Move Emma to another room. I don't want to cause her any problems."

Charlotte frowned at Lawrence and then shook her head.

"Your consideration for our reputations is overwhelming, my lord. How was I lucky enough to marry you? I hope Emma enjoys the fruits of my labour."

She swept out of the room to give the orders to return her possessions to her bedroom and place Emma's belongings in the room previously occupied by Lawrence's mistress. Barrington grinned when he heard the instructions relating to the room that Emma was to inhabit. He admired Charlotte because, while she was subtle, she could still make her point. Emma, staying in the former mistress's room, spoke volumes.

Chapter Twenty-Six

WHEN BARRINGTON ANNOUNCED dinner, Charlotte inspected herself again in the mirror and headed for her door. Molly had spent extra time tonight preparing her mistress. She had pulled Charlotte's curls to one side and arranged them in an upswept style.

"You look lovely, my lady. The earl will see you tonight and wonder why he is pursuing that sister of yours."

Charlotte smiled at her abigail.

"I doubt that, but I'm pleased to have fashionable clothes. I feel no guilt at spending the Earl's money."

As Charlotte approached the dining room, Barrington stepped forward and opened the door. She smiled her thanks as she entered the room. The other diners sat at the table.

"Sorry if I held up the meal. I lost track of time."

Phillip rose from the table, his face wreathed in smiles.

"Charlotte, you look lovely tonight. That gown is stunning."

Charlotte chuckled and gave a small curtsy.

"Thank you, Phillip. I adore the colour of this gown; it is my favourite of all the dresses I had the seamstress make." She leaned closer and whispered, "You will pay for them, won't you?"

Phillip laughed. "Yes, I will. The seamstress deserves every penny she charged."

Emma glared at Lawrence. "You said she had ugly gowns. That gown looks new."

The whining voice of her sister set Charlotte's teeth on edge, but before she could respond, Lawrence spoke.

"What happened to the ugly brown dress you were wearing, Charlotte? Where did that dress and your riding habit come from?"

"I tossed out the ugly dresses. This dress is one of a wardrobe full of clothes I had made for myself in Windemere while you were away."

Lawrence frowned. "You spent a fortune on clothes?"

"Yes, I did. When you send me away, I have no intention of only having two ugly gowns and a night rail to my name. You worry that my sister might not like the estate, but the one she sees now is all thanks to the hard work of the staff, the villagers, and me. I worked as hard as the crofters, and I deserve compensation. You, my lord, have not even thanked me for my work, so I paid myself."

Charlotte glowered at her husband. He had the good grace to stay quiet, but Emma had no qualms and launched an attack.

"You stole money from Lawrence? Maybe he should call the local constable to take you away. I will not have you frittering away money that belongs to his lordship. When we marry, we will need the funds to live as the leading family in the district. I can't imagine why you need extra clothes. You will return to running the household at our father's house, the same as before coming here."

Charlotte turned to Barrington, who stood with the other servers.

"Barrington, do you think I should encourage Emma to change her gown?"

Barrington spluttered, attempting to turn his laugh into a cough. The young servers grinned at the suggestion. Lawrence pinned a glare at his wife.

"I will tan your hide if you even lean towards the vase."

Charlotte shrugged and turned her attention to her sister.

"I always knew you were selfish, but I didn't think you were delusional. Call the local constable and tell him Lady Charlotte spent her husband's money on clothes. He'll laugh you out of the room. Oh, I will not return to our father's house."

"Where will you go?" Emma and Lawrence spoke at the same time.

Charlotte gave a slight smile. "Once you two marry, my whereabouts will be none of your business."

After the uncomfortable meal finished and the diners dispersed, Charlotte went to the library. As she sat in the silent room, she fretted about her future. It was all very well to spin a tale to her sister and her husband; it differed from finding a home. Phillip's knock on the door interrupted her thoughts.

"Am I intruding, Charlotte?"

"No, I am always eager for a normal conversation with you. Sanity is in short supply in this household. Even though I told Lawrence I wouldn't live with my father, it was bravado. When he ends our marriage, my options seem to be the poorhouse or a stable somewhere. After staying here for six months, it will ruin my reputation when the ton discovers Lawrence has annulled our marriage. I have no home and no prospects, and my last days here are to be marred by my sister's presence."

"We discussed the issue with your parents, and Lawrence offered to find you a husband by increasing your dowry. He thought a gentleman with pockets to let might wed you."

"Damn the cad, so he is happy to pay someone to take me off his hands. We both know what kind of gentleman will take a ruined spinster for a wife. I will be married to a wastrel like my father, and every time the bounder gets angry or drunk, he'll harass me about my ruined reputation. No, thank you. If Lawrence wants to throw money around, he can set me up in a cottage somewhere."

"I understand your reluctance to marry someone Lawrence pays, but there is another choice. When my mother was alone at my small estate a while ago, you offered her a companion and the dower house. Emma sent a message telling my Mother and Peggy they are not welcome to stay in the house, and that Mother won't stay where she is unwelcome. Mother said that once Emma and Lawrence marry, she will move back to our smallholding. The house is large enough to accommodate you and Molly if you wish to live there."

"It would be an honour to share the house, as long as that is acceptable to your mother."

"My mother offered her home when she heard Lawrence intended to dissolve the marriage and marry Emma. She wants to repay your kindness."

"I will walk over to the dowager's house and thank her before organising a groom to ride with me tomorrow morning."

The walk to the dowager's house was only a short distance, and Charlotte wanted to ensure that Mrs Hilderbrand was happy with the prospect of her moving into the family home. When Phillip's mother opened the door, the smile she gave Charlotte warmed her heart.

"Come in, Dear. It's good to see you."

As the ladies chatted, Mrs Hilderbrand's companion arrived with a pot of tea and some pastries. Charlotte raised the conversation she had with Phillip, and his Mother immediately reissued the invitation to join her when Lawrence married Emma.

"If you don't mind me saying, but Lord Clayhurst is a fool. I haven't met your sister, but the tone of the letter she sent to give me my marching orders smacked of snobbery. Why would Lord Clayhurst want a spiteful piece of work like her when he could marry a kind, attractive, hard-working woman? It defies logic."

Charlotte had no answer for that question.

Chapter Twenty-Seven

MOLLY UNTIED CHARLOTTE'S laces and helped her remove her garments to prepare for sleep. Once Charlotte doused the lights, the only illumination in the room was from the banked fire. The conversation over the dinner table riled Charlotte. What had happened to her sister? When had she become so money-hungry? It wasn't as if her father denied her whatever she wanted during her time at their parents' house. Any money that their father accumulated went to Emma for clothes and social outings. Charlotte rolled over, determined to sleep despite the ugly scene that evening.

A knock on the connecting door roused Charlotte from her sleep.

"Charlotte, open the door."

Charlotte slid out of bed and walked to the door.

"What do you want?"

"Open the door; I want to talk to you."

His eyes slowly swept Charlotte when Lawrence walked through the door. Her blood rose, and she crossed her arms.

"What do you want?"

"I'm sorry that the circumstances of our marriage must distress you. I did not intend to upset you."

"Distressing? What rubbish you speak. You had no thoughts of how this might affect me. All you can think of is besting my father and having a lovely wife so that other men will be jealous. It's funny how that has worked out; the only men who know what you're doing are Phillip and Barrington, and neither envies you."

Charlotte turned her back on her husband.

"Lawrence, get out. I don't need your platitudes. I want this finished so I can get on with my life."

The earl stared at Charlotte.

"Have you got a prospective husband chosen?"

"What if I have? Why do you care what I do once you finish with me? Phillip told me that you would sell me to the first hard-up man who takes your money. You would return me to the same homelife I thought I escaped when my Father ordered me to marry you. I will be tied to a drunkard and a gambler, and instead of it being my Father, it will be my husband. God, you have no shame and no integrity. You and Emma are welcome to each other; she has no integrity or shame, either. You two should be a good match. I regret that Phillip was the proxy and not the groom. He is decent and has integrity, two things you lack."

Charlotte and Lawrence stood toe to toe, trading insults and hurtful comments. Suddenly, Lawrence hooked his hand behind Charlotte's neck and pulled her towards him. As she opened her mouth to speak, his lips descended on hers. She closed her mouth and held her breath, but she was no match for his skill. He teased her with butterfly kisses, then used his tongue and lips to caress hers. He nibbled on her bottom lip and soothed the sting with his tongue.

"Open your mouth, Charlotte."

As she grabbed the front of his shirt, her lips parted. Despite the angst that this man caused her, he would always have a hold over her.

The kisses were exquisite; even the first time Lawrence had kissed her paled in comparison. Her head felt dizzy, and her skin heated from his touch. She feared she might pass out when he pulled her hair to one side and feasted on her neck. He pushed her chemise off her shoulders. His kisses moved from her neck to the tops of her breasts.

Charlotte struggled to stay standing. Lawrence's breathing had become laboured, and the look in his eyes turned Charlotte's knees to water. When he pulled her chemise aside to expose her breasts,

Charlotte had a moment of pleasure at the admiration in his eyes. He groaned and lavished her breasts with his talented hands and mouth. In an instant, Lawrence transferred them to her bed. Charlotte never knew what could be pleasurable between a man and a woman. The heat and tingling in her breasts spread all over her body. She squirmed and rubbed herself against Lawrence. She needed more, although she didn't know what that more was.

Lawrence ran his hand along Charlotte's leg, scrunching her nightgown as his hand moved higher. Charlotte groaned; the feel of Lawrence's hand as he explored her body made Charlotte shudder. Her face flamed with shame as she remembered Lawrence's comments about wanton women. Before she could control her body's reaction to her husband's foreplay, someone tapped at Lawrence's door; Charlotte was so enthralled in the sensations the earl created that she paid no heed to the sound.

"Lawrence, open the door."

Charlotte froze at her sister's voice, and the earl groaned as he moved away. He walked through the adjoining door, straightening his clothes as he went, and pulled it behind him. Left alone on the bed, Charlotte covered herself and shivered. As the tears welled in her eyes, she padded to the adjoining door. Through the gap, Charlotte could see Lawrence and Emma locked in each other's arms, kissing. She pulled the door closed and locked it.

Her shame at being taken in by the Earl's ruse overwhelmed her. How could she think he was ready to consummate their marriage? His desertion of her when her sister called him humiliated her. Was this how her life was to go? It was plain to her now; Lawrence would marry Emma and give her children, and she would be his mistress, and any offspring of hers would be illegitimate. Disgusted with her naivete, Charlotte scrubbed herself in the water Molly had left for her morning wash. She was desperate to remove the earl's touch and smell from her skin.

The night was endless. Charlotte tossed and turned, reliving the encounter with the earl. The sensations Lawrence evoked by touching her were both unfamiliar and enjoyable. Sadness washed through her as she thought of never having her husband in her bed again. They consumed her when the tears came, and she gave in to the despair that swept through her.

Knowing that her husband went straight from her bed to her sister's felt like a dagger piercing her heart. When she was sent here after her sham wedding, she thought that life couldn't get any worse than living with her father. How wrong she had been. At her Father's house, the neglect and jibes about her origin had been occurring for so long that even though they hurt, Charlotte shrugged them off. However, Laurence's callous disregard for her future was exacerbated by his dalliance with her and subsequent abandonment.

Chapter Twenty-Eight

WHEN CHARLOTTE WOKE the following day, her eyes felt gritty, and her face was puffy. Her head ached, and the dull thump in her temples made leaving her bed harder than usual. Charlotte eased from the bed and struggled into her riding habit; she was not ready to face Lawrence over the breakfast table.

Molly met Charlotte on the stairs, and her distress at Charlotte's ravaged face was instant.

"My lady, you are unwell? You should return to bed, and I will bring hot chocolate."

"No thanks, Molly. A ride will clear my head. I'll eat breakfast later."

As Charlotte left the house, Barrington glanced at Molly, who stood watching her mistress walk away. He shook his head in distress.

"What has the master done this time? It has to be him or that sister of hers."

"I don't know. Lady Charlotte had dressed when I got to her room. A ride will relieve her of the awkwardness of facing the earl and his intended at the breakfast table, but I'm concerned for her. "

Henry saw Charlotte leave the house, her face puffy, eyes red, and shoulders slumped. While the groom hitched the carriage horse to the cart for his morning pick-up run, he collected the horse Charlotte rode and threw her saddle onto it. He helped her onto her horse when she approached and hustled the grooms to hurry them.

"Who will go with me today?"

"Well, that's a problem."

"What, you can't spare someone to keep me company?"

"Ah, his lordship said he doesn't want to pay a groom who spends half the day doing nothing. He said that as long as you stay on the estate, you won't need a groom to keep you company."

Charlotte ducked her head as the tears fell again.

"What was I thinking, taking a groom with me each morning?"

Henry observed his mistress with concern. This morning, something was wrong; her cheerful outlook and smile were absent today. What could have made her so unhappy? He might know what to do if he had time to speak with Barrington before the ride.

They rode in silence, and the village was in sight before long.

"Are you intending to ride back with me or stay in the village for a while, Lady Charlotte?"

"I want to check on little Paul. His mother said he developed a cough, so I'll ride back later."

"Are you coming straight back? Should I send a groom to meet you?"

Charlotte gave Henry a wan smile. "What, and risk the wrath of the Earl? No, I'll ride through the fields on the eastern side of the estate on my way home. I will be fine, but you'd best get on your way, or Mrs Hatton will be cross at her worker's late arrival."

Henry nodded and stepped from the cart to lift Charlotte from the sidesaddle. He handed the horse to one of the teenage boys who gathered when the carriage arrived, and the youth moved away to tether the horse. Henry watched Charlotte with concern. He knew that her visit to the workers was not unusual, but he also knew it was a way of avoiding the trouble at the manor house.

When Lawrence walked into the breakfast room, the sight of Emma and Phillip ignoring each other greeted him.

"What the devil is wrong with you two, and where is Charlotte?"

"I don't know where Charlotte is, and I may have to share the table with Emma, but I don't have to enjoy it."

"Barrington, where the devil is Charlotte?"

The butler eyed his master with distaste.

"Lady Charlotte rose early and rode to the village with Henry. She was very distressed."

Emma glared at the butler.

"Barrington, you know you must stop calling her Lady Charlotte when I marry the earl?"

"Yes, madame, as you wish."

Once Barrington left the room, Emma turned her ire on Lawrence.

"Why do you let that stuffed shirt talk to me that way? I will give him his marching orders when I'm the mistress here. That Mrs Hatton will go too, and we will need a French chef, not a cook, for our social events."

"Emma, they are my staff, and I will make any changes necessary."

Emma fluttered her eyes at the Earl.

"Don't be foolish, Lawrence. It would be best if you oversaw the outside staff, and your wife must organise the household staff. Although I don't understand why you give Charlotte free rein with the staff, it is beyond me. She treats them all as friends, and they show no respect."

"Yes, well, she has no problems with the staff. There is work to catch up on, so I will be in my study." Lawrence stood and bowed to Emma as he made his way out of the room.

Once he closed the door behind himself, Lawrence ran his hands through his hair and groaned. Once he sat in his favourite chair, he sorted through the morning's accounts. Barrington's hostile frame of mind was clear, and Charlotte's distress caused his hostility. Barrington was an excellent judge of people; he was visibly distraught upon seeing Charlotte's anguish. Lawrence knew he was the cause of her sadness.

How the hell did he get into this mess? If Emma hadn't interrupted last night, he wouldn't have stopped when he did. Lawrence knew he had caused Charlotte's distress; his treatment of her was appalling. Lawrence bolted from the bed when Emma called and raced into his room. If he had let Emma catch him in compromising circumstances with Charlotte, it would cause untold havoc. He left Charlotte frustrated and confused. She must have seen Emma's kisses because the open door between the two rooms was quietly closed, and the lock was activated. His wish for revenge had skewed his judgment, and instead of seeing Charlotte for who she was, he fixated on her sister.

The first kiss he shared with Charlotte scared him into ridiculing her the next day, prompting him to run off to London. Last night's kisses swept away his sanity; all he wanted was more of the woman who infuriated and intrigued him. Charlotte's kisses were untutored but sweet and passionate, while Emma's were practised and lacked passion. How could he saddle himself with a mean-spirited woman when he was married to the warm, joyful sister? Unravelling the mess he had created was going to take time and skill.

Loud bashing on the door and shouts interrupted the earl's pondering. He raced out into the hall, almost colliding with Emma as he reached the foot of the stairs. Barrington looked upset, and Henry was yelling for the Earl.

"What is the meaning of this, Barrington? Since when did the hired help go to the front door?" screeched Emma.

"Hush up, Emma. What has got you all upset, Henry?" Lawrence asked.

"My lord, I am sorry to disturb you, but Lady Charlotte's horse has just galloped into the stables with the saddle hanging. Lady Charlotte has taken a tumble, and we must look for her. I am organising the stable hands-on horseback and will take the cart. I thought we should inform you."

"Goodness, all this fuss is for nothing! Charlotte falls all the time. You are overreacting; she will walk in here in another while and be none the worse for wear."

"We are ready to go, your lordship. Do you wish to come too?"

"No, he doesn't want to waste time on a pointless exercise. Run along if you must; his lordship has pressing business."

Lawrence stood mute, trying to decide on the best course of action. Did Charlotte fall off the horse often? Why didn't she and Henry buy a safer mount if that was the case? He'd watched her ride into the stables many times, and it didn't appear that the horse frightened her. Indeed, if you fell off the same horse innumerable times, you would show uneasiness. But she was animated and happy each time he saw Charlotte on the same bay horse. While he pondered these questions, Henry gave up waiting for an answer and left the house.

When Lawrence looked up, it was to see Barrington's glare. Molly and Mrs Hatton shared expressions of disappointment. Lawrence looked to see Phillip's reaction and realised that Phillip was gone, too.

"Mrs Hatton, ask the cook to prepare afternoon tea." Emma's expressionless announcement left Lawrence stunned. How could Emma shrug it off if her sister was hurt, as was Henry's expectation regarding the riderless horse? Was she completely heartless? Lawrence remembered Phillip's information about where Charlotte's clothes came from and Emma's unwillingness to share. It seemed he had made a deal with the devil, and it would take some trouble extracting himself from this mess of his own making.

Chapter Twenty-Nine

THE WAIT FELT ENDLESS. Lawrence paced back and forward, his gaze drawn to the sitting-room window. Emma chastised him for his melodramatics, but the longer he waited, the more Lawrence cursed himself for not going with the riders. Lawrence rushed to the front door when the sound of a cantering horse filtered through to the drawing room. As Barrington opened the door, Ben, the groom Charlotte often rode with, barrelled into the entryway.

"Mr Phillip said to have Molly and Mrs Hatton ready to help. Young Simon has ridden for the doctor, and Henry is bringing Lady Charlotte back in the cart."

The cart stopped at the front door, and Phillip jumped from his horse. He scooped Charlotte up from the wagon's bed and rushed towards the door. One of the grooms collected the abandoned horses, but the rest of the searchers pushed into the hallway behind Phillip.

Emma watched as Phillip carried Charlotte into the house.

"For goodness' sake, Hilderbrand, put her on the ground and let her walk."

Phillip shook his head. "She is unconscious, you stupid woman."

Emma glared at Phillip.

"Mrs Hatton, find the smelling salts so my sister can come out of her faint."

As Phillip ascended the stairs, he said, "Molly, get the bandages and salve, and Mrs Hatton, get a bowl of warm water that we might use to clean the cuts and grazes."

Molly raced back to the stairs, and Emma blocked her path.

"Please move; we are treating your sister."

"You insolent baggage! I gave you an instruction."

Molly shoved Emma out of the way. "Why don't you and the earl return to your afternoon tea and let the people who love Mistress Charlotte treat her?"

Suddenly, Lawrence came out of his daze.

"Molly, go to Charlotte's bedroom. Emma, finish your afternoon tea, and I will see if I can help."

"You will help? Why on earth bother?"

"Because she is my wife, that's why."

When Lawrence entered Charlotte's room, Phillip had laid her on the bed.

"We need to remove her habit to gauge her injuries. Molly, come over here, and I will sit Charlotte up while you unlace and unbutton her clothes."

Lawrence intervened. "No, she is my wife, and I will help undress her. Phillip, you may wait in the hall, and I will call you when we have her in a chemise."

Lawrence lifted Charlotte and rested her head against his shoulder while Molly unbuttoned and unlaced the habit and eased it forward, one arm at a time. Lawrence laid Charlotte on the bed and pulled the bodice from his wife's torso. He raised her as Molly lifted the attached skirt over Charlotte's head.

"Molly, use the water Mrs Hatton brought in and bathe Charlotte's face and the abrasions on her hands and knees. Be careful of her left arm; I'm sure she has broken it."

"Yes, Lord Clayhurst."

As Molly bathed Charlotte, Lawrence opened the door to the doctor. Phillip entered the room, but the doctor evicted the men. Lawrence paced the length of the hallway, all the while cursing himself. This accident would not have happened if he hadn't refused to allow a groom to ride with Charlotte. Even if the accident had occurred, someone would have been with her.

"This is your fault," Phillip accused.

"Maybe. But why was the girth loose enough to allow the saddle to roll?"

"Who knows? Your wife is lying unconscious because you refused to allow the groom to ride with her. You want to hope she wakes up because you can't marry your sister-in-law if Charlotte dies. That would mess up your life."

Phillip didn't see the fist until it struck him in the face. As he staggered back, he grabbed his jaw.

"What, the truth doesn't sound as rosy anymore?"

"Phillip, unless you want me to hit you again, I suggest you shut your mouth."

The doctor's arrival at the door ended the fisticuffs.

"Lord Clayhurst, I need splints for your wife's arm. Could you have someone organise that?"

When the groom raced off to the yard to find pieces of wood for the splint, Lawrence sighed.

"Henry, you and the other staff may return to your posts. I will inform you of Charlotte's condition when the doctor leaves."

"Yes, my lord."

"Oh, Henry, see if you can find out how the girth came loose on my wife's horse."

Henry nodded and walked away. Lawrence was under no illusion that Henry would carry out the instruction for him, but the man would investigate what happened because of his fondness for Charlotte. But at the moment, the cause of the accident wasn't as crucial as Charlotte's well-being, and Lawrence would do whatever it took to aid her recovery.

Lawrence thought about what Phillip had said as he waited for the doctor to allow him entrance to the sick room. He and Emma couldn't marry if Charlotte died; it was against the law to marry your sister-in-law, but he had no desire to marry Emma. How he would extricate himself from this mess would have to wait until he saw how Charlotte fared.

Charlotte looked small and frail as she lay motionless in the bed. Molly wanted to sit with her mistress, but Lawrence had sent her to organise a pallet for the bedroom. Molly could sleep next to Charlotte at night, and then he and Mrs Hatton could take turns in the daytime. Phillip offered to sit with Charlotte, but Lawrence, angry at his friend's accurate assessment of the state of affairs, refused.

Days passed, and Charlotte did not wake. The doctor's prognosis that she would die if she didn't wake soon ate at Lawrence's consciousness. His decision to stop the groom from accompanying Charlotte and his behaviour the night before had led to this tragedy. The entire thing was his fault. If Charlotte woke, could she ever forgive him?

The door opening interrupted his angst.

"Lawrence, what are you doing? We should hurry back to London so you can annul the marriage. If Charlotte dies before...."

"Get out!" Lawrence shouted.

Emma stepped back.

"Are you mad, woman? What man could discard his wife as she lay ill in bed?"

"Well, if you leave it too late, we cannot marry."

"Maybe that wouldn't be a bad thing."

Emma huffed at Lawrence and stormed out of the room.

Lawrence shook his head. How had he thought Emma was a better choice for a wife than Charlotte? Phillip had seen Charlotte's worth right from the start, while Lawrence was too busy focusing on payback. Lawrence intended to return Emma to London if Charlotte regained consciousness in the next few days. He would introduce her to a few fellows with titles or money and leave her to her own devices. Emma was interested in his wealth and would transfer her attention to any wealthy man who showed an interest in her. Charlotte had captured the hearts of his staff and the local tenants with her kindness and warmth. Earlier, Lawrence hadn't wanted to admit that he had fallen under her spell. But as her life hung in the balance, he realised he would miss her if she died. God, this mess was all his fault, and he prayed that she would wake soon so he could rectify the injustice he had caused her. The alternative didn't bear considering.

As the day wore on, Lawrence became more agitated. He patted Charlotte's cheeks and hands, attempting to rouse her. Fear gripped him, and his chest felt like it was in a vice. When dinner time arrived, he changed places with Molly and went to the dining room for the evening meal. For Lawrence, sitting with Phillip and Emma was a torment. Emma never let up about their marriage, and Phillip sat, silently berating Lawrence. Towards the end of the meal, Barrington announced that Henry was outside and wished to speak with Lawrence.

"Send him in, please, Barrington. We will talk here. Pull up another chair for him."

Emma's horrified gasp had Barrington halting in his spot.

"Lawrence, what is wrong with you? Interrupting your meal to speak with a stable hand is uncouth, but how could you subject your fiancé to the indignity of sharing a table with a worker? It is an outrage."

Lawrence shrugged. "If you don't wish to mix with the world's workers, you may leave the table. Barrington, do as I ask."

Emma glared at Lawrence. "You will regret your decision, my lord," she said as she flounced from the room.

Lawrence watched the spoiled younger daughter of his debtor flounce from the room. Did she ever think of anyone but herself? He glanced across at Phillip, who sat with a smile on his face. Hadn't Phillip told him that Emma would make his life miserable? Rather than concede, he focused on the intrusion of his stable master.

When Henry entered the room, Lawrence gestured towards a chair.

"What is so important that you have to interrupt my meal?"

"I have found out why Mistress Charlotte's saddle came loose."

"Well, spit it out."

"When Lady Charlotte and I arrived at the village, I handed the horse to one of the young blokes. He loosened off the girth because he didn't know how long Mistress Charlotte would be. He wasn't there when she remounted, and the lad who helped her mount didn't think to check how tight the girth was."

Lawrence hung his head. "Damnation! It's my fault the mix-up occurred. This mishap wouldn't have happened if I had sent her with a groom. How many times has she ridden to the village without mishap? Many times, I guess, but always with a groom."

After he pushed back his chair, Lawrence strode to the sideboard. He splashed a large dash of whisky into a glass and downed the contents in one gulp. His mood was shattered at the sound of a woman's shout. Molly burst into the room.

"My lord, Mistress Charlotte is awake."

"Thank the lord," he said as he raced for the door.

With Phillip following behind, Lawrence raced up the stairs. His hand reached towards the door of Charlotte's room, and he hesitated. He stepped back.

"I'm the last person on earth she wishes to see. You go in, Phillip. It will please her to see you, and you can relay how she is to me."

Without hesitation, Phillip entered the room. Charlotte looked fragile. Her pasty white skin stretched over her prominent cheekbones. A skeletal hand lay on the coverlet, and her glossy hair hung in clumps around her shoulders.

"Dear God, Charlotte. You scared us all to death. Molly has gone to the kitchen to fetch broth, and you must try to eat. Any thinner, my dear, and you will fade away to a shadow."

Once Molly arrived with the broth, Phillip excused himself and searched for Lawrence. He found him in the breakfast room, accompanied by Emma. They were in an angry discussion. Lawrence broke off what he was saying and glanced up at Phillip.

"How is she?"

Phillip shook his head. "She may be awake, but not out of danger yet, from how she looks. Charlotte has lost so much weight in the intervening days that, even if she had wanted to stand, I doubt she has the strength. Her recovery will take weeks, if not months."

"Should I hire a nurse for her?"

Phillip rubbed his chin. "If you do, you will offend Molly and Mrs Hatton. Have the doctor check Charlotte daily for the first few weeks, and as she mends, he could visit less often."

Emma stood and moved towards the door.

"Heavens, if you two intend to fuss over Charlotte, I have better things to do with my time."

Neither man commented as Emma flounced out of the room.

Chapter Thirty

DAY AFTER DAY, CHARLOTTE lay in bed. As she gained weight, she felt more capable of engaging in brief conversations. Sitting up tired her, and the thought of getting out of bed was daunting. The doctor visited daily and pronounced his pleasure at her progress. Charlotte could have visitors by the doctor's ruling, but he limited their time to a few minutes. Any more, and he feared Charlotte might relapse.

Charlotte's heart leapt each time the door opened; would the visitor this time be Lawrence? But Charlotte was disappointed each time her visitors showed themselves. It appeared as though Lawrence cared so little for his wife that he couldn't check her himself. The one visitor that Charlotte didn't want to see was her sister. Unfortunately for her, the very visitor she wished not to see strolled into her room one afternoon.

"Molly, you can leave us. I'll call you when I leave."

Molly glanced at Charlotte and prepared to leave upon receiving a wan smile.

"The doctor said visitors are not to stay too long, Miss Emma."

"Phooey! I'll stay as long as I need. Now go along, girl. I have things to discuss with your mistress."

When Molly closed the door, Emma scrutinised Charlotte.

"God, any wonder your husband doesn't want you. Your hair hangs in rats' tails, and I swear you smell. The good thing that comes from this debacle is that it has firmed up Lawrence's decision to resolve the problem you and our father perpetuated."

"I had nothing to do with the ruse father pulled on Lawrence, and you know it. You were there when he announced who was to be Lawrence's bride. Are you so delusional that you can't recall the facts? Even though I challenged my father, he gave the money meant for my clothes to you. Did you spend any of it on the servants, or are they still wearing old garments? Why are you in my room? What do you want?"

Emma laughed. "What irony. You worked like a commoner, and now the estate is fit for Lawrence and me to inhabit. We are going to the city now that you won't die. Lawrence says we will be away for a month. Make sure you're gone before we get back."

Charlotte didn't believe what she was hearing. Had Lawrence postponed the trip to ensure she didn't die and prevent him from marrying Emma? Why couldn't he visit her to tell her what was happening himself instead of letting her nasty sister impart the news?

Molly bustled back into the room just as Emma prepared to leave.

"I told you I would call you when I was ready. Why are you intruding?"

"The doctor said only quick visits. I'm sorry if you haven't finished your discussion with Lady Charlotte, but your time has finished."

"When Lady Charlotte leaves, you will be part of my staff. It would bode well for you to show respect, girl, or you will find yourself in the streets."

Molly smiled thinly. "I'd prefer to be out in the streets than work for you. A woman who treats her sister the way you have would be horrible to her staff. I will leave with Lady Charlotte when she goes, so you needn't worry about me."

Emma gave a brief laugh. "Ha. You will both be in the workhouse. A fitting end to this whole saga."

With that parting shot, Emma waltzed out of the room.

Molly helped Charlotte lie back against the pillows.

"Pardon me saying, miss, but that sister of yours is a nasty piece of work. I can't understand the Earl preferring her to you."

"Well, he does. Emma just gave me my marching orders. They are going to the city for a month, and when they return, we will have to be gone. Once they leave, I'll get the doctor to check me, and we'll move to Phillip's place as soon as possible."

Charlotte slumped in her bed. She knew why Lawrence had chosen Emma. The sisters were so different. Emma was petite and elegant, with blond hair always styled in the latest fashion, and her clothes showcased her assets. In contrast, Charlotte was taller and had a fuller figure than her sister. Charlotte's hair was thick and curly, and she either wore it loose or had Molly bundle it into a bun to keep it out of the way. When it came to appearances, Charlotte had nothing to offer Lawrence.

Charlotte kept returning to the two intimate encounters she had shared with Lawrence. Did they mean nothing to him? The kisses and caresses burned into Charlotte's brain, and she could do nothing to remove them. Charlotte had no other kisses to measure against Lawrence's, but to her inexperienced self, they were perfect. He had said so many hurtful things that she should be able to push him from her mind, but it was not something that she could do. All she could do now was to recover, and when she and Molly moved to Mrs Hilderbrand's house, she could make some decisions about her future. But for the moment, the options were limited. With her reputation ruined, even the possibility of becoming a governess was unlikely.

Chapter Thirty-One

FOUR WEEKS LATER

Barrington heard a rider coming hell-for-leather down the driveway. He strolled to the door, preparing to open it for the speeding visitor. Barrington stepped back, shocked at seeing the earl in such a state of dishevelment. When the earl returned, the last thing Barrington expected was for him to arrive alone.

"My lord, your arrival is unexpected. We had no warning of your arrival. You have no luggage?"

Lawrence pulled off his cravat and stuffed it in his pocket.

"The carriage is behind me, but I was tired of the time it was taking. My bags are with the carriage. Ask the footmen to prepare me a bath, and I will change before dinner."

"Yes, my lord."

"Oh, and inform my wife of my arrival."

Barrington's bewildered stare made Lawrence mutter.

"My wife, Barrington. Is that too much to ask?"

"Pardon me, my lord, but isn't Miss Emma in the carriage?"

"Not Emma, you fool! Tell Lady Charlotte that I have arrived. I will talk to her after I bathe."

"My lord, Lady Charlotte, is not here."

"Damn, I should have sent a message. When will my wife return?"

Barrington scrutinised his employer. The man must be mad. Why would Lady Charlotte stay after his lordship returned with a new wife?

"She won't return, sir. Miss Emma gave Lady Charlotte and Mrs Hilderbrand their marching orders before returning to town. Mrs Hilderbrand left at once. Lady Charlotte needed more recuperation time and didn't leave until last week."

She left?"

"Yes, sir. Did you expect Lady Charlotte to stay to watch you with another wife?"

Barrington's look of disdain at him made Lawrence hot under the collar.

"I didn't marry Emma. She and I returned to London to attend social events. I hoped she could find other suitors. Two fellows courted her when I left, so she should make a suitable match. Where the hell did my wife go?"

"I don't know, your lord. She was very secretive, even using carriage drivers from elsewhere. I don't think she wants anyone to discover her whereabouts. Why did Miss Emma tell Lady Charlotte to leave if she didn't expect to return as the mistress?"

"Because I didn't tell her I was not ending my marriage. She would have refused to leave if she had known of my intentions before we were in the city. I thought it was safer to play along for the time being. It never occurred to me that Charlotte would leave."

Barrington remained mute, mulling over how stupid his lordship was. The man married the perfect wife. She was beautiful and kind, and her hard work and vision restored his property. What more could a man want? But he chose the flashy sister, only to discover the glitz covered a nasty disposition.

"Damn it. Get my bath organised, and I'll think of what to do when I've eaten. There must be a way to find where she went."

Lawrence sat at the table, his meal in front of him. As he ate, his brain mulled over the predicament before him. Who would know of Charlotte's whereabouts? Molly would, but he had seen no evidence of her when he returned. Did she go with Charlotte? Did Phillip know about Charlotte's location? Assuming that the annulment was legal, would Charlotte and Phillip become involved? The two were as thick as thieves, and Phillip stuck up for Charlotte, even from the start of the debacle that was his marriage. The meal congealed in Lawrence's stomach, and he pushed the plate away.

That night, Lawrence slept fitfully. Memories of what he said to Charlotte and the disdain with which he treated her kept him awake for most of the night. The memories of his two intimate moments with Charlotte caused him to cringe. He knew she was innocent the first time he kissed Charlotte, but her unbridled response made him lose his head. The second time he had been alone with Charlotte, he knew he would have consummated the marriage had Emma not intervened. Why had it taken her accident for him to realise that his wife had become important to him?

Lawrence rose the following day, feeling tired and out of sorts. After deciding that he would summon Phillip in the early hours of the morning, he dozed while waiting for the sun to rise. Lawrence cursed himself for getting caught up in his revenge, only realising his mistake as Charlotte lay injured. Why didn't he tell her he had changed his mind and that the trip to the city was to rectify his wrongdoings toward the sisters? Would she have remained here if she knew she would live with him, and Emma was no longer part of the picture?

Lawrence roamed the estate for the next week, checking on progress with crops and the townsfolk. His reception from the residents was not as fulsome as on his first visit. As Lawrence moved through the village, the livestock on one of the cropping fields confused him. Dismounting from his horse, he tied his mount to a hitching post and called to one old-timer who often sat outside his home.

"Davy, what's happening with the stock? Even though the area is small, they are still on cropping land."

Davy levered his aging body out of the chair and walked towards Lawrence. He bowed and said, "Mistress Charlotte saw the need for the townsfolk to be less dependent on the estate's crops. Our men work in the fields, but our kids go hungry if the crop fails or yields less than expected. The idea surfaced when she gave the kids the old pony. She checked on him most days to ensure the kids fed and watered him, and it spread from there."

Lawrence rubbed his chin. Trust Charlotte to tackle a problem with logic and sense.

"I can see two cows, chickens and vegetables. Who takes care of the jobs? How do you stop the arguments over who gets the food?"

Davy pointed to the extensive area planted with vegetables.

"Lady Charlotte had the younger men set up the vegetable plots. Now, the womenfolk weed and upkeep them. People are free to take what they want. The produce is always available, so they take just what they need for the day. Youngsters milk the cows, and they also feed the chickens. The girls collect eggs daily and place them with the milk pitchers on the table over yonder."

No wonder the people here revered Charlotte; her poor treatment must make it hard for locals to talk to him. He must find his wife and make up for his unacceptable behaviour. While these people were his tenants, Charlotte owned their hearts.

Chapter Thirty-Two

BARRINGTON ANNOUNCED Phillip, and Lawrence rose from his seat when his man of business walked into the room. Phillip's eyebrows shot up, and his mouth gaped open.

"What the hell happened to you?"

"My wife left me."

"How could she leave you? You only just married the nasty-tongued vixen."

Lawrence looked at Phillip as though he'd lost his reason.

"Not Emma, you fool, Charlotte. Charlotte has left me."

"Well, excuse me if I appear simple, but isn't that what you always wanted? She's done you a favour, and now you can go on with your new life as though nothing untoward happened. You should be happy with the outcome. Did you believe that, after how you and Emma treated Charlotte, she would stay so you could humiliate her some more?"

Lawrence shot up from his chair and stalked over to the bottle of whisky sitting on the sideboard. He sloshed a dash into a glass and tossed it back in one gulp.

"I have just had this conversation with Barrington, but he trod more warily than you. When I left, I took Emma back to the city and spent four endless weeks introducing her to titled men with money. The plan was to have some unfortunate sod offer for her before showing her true nature. I left her, trying to choose between a wealthy baron and a rich duke. When I left here the last time, I didn't intend to marry Emma. Before the accident, I realised I had married the right woman."

Phillip poured himself a drink and then rounded on Lawrence.

"Did it occur to you at any stage to tell Charlotte what you were doing? When her sister ordered my mother and her companion to vacate the dowager house, she also said Charlotte had to leave before you, and she returned. Well, the women are all gone. If you have changed your plan, you will need to apologise. I'm not sure an apology will help, but you can only try."

"How can I apologise? I don't know where she is. Do you?"

"Well, I just might. Who says Charlotte will want to see you?"

"Damn it, Phillip! Tell me where she is."

"I'll tell you what. I will visit Charlotte, and if she wants you to visit, I will return for you. That's the best I can do. If I leave in the morning, I should return in two days."

When Phillip trotted away the day after, Lawrence considered following him. His man of business had headed towards the front gate, but he could turn either way once the drive intersected with the road. It would be tricky to follow close enough not to get lost, but if Phillip suspected someone was following, he would take Lawrence to task. Lawrence put thoughts of following Phillip out of his mind. Soon, he should be able to see Charlotte and rectify the mess he had made of their marriage.

The next few days were the longest in Lawrence's life. Doubts assailed him at every turn, and he felt as though he was going mad. Would Charlotte allow him to call on her? What if he apologised and she didn't accept his explanation? What if she couldn't forgive him? It would lock him in a marriage where he wanted Charlotte, but she wanted nothing to do with him.

When the sound of Phillip's hoof beats reached the study, Lawrence stopped himself from draining the remains of the bottle of whisky. Phillip entered the room, dusty and dishevelled from his ride.

"I need to clean up, but I will put you out of your misery. I explained the reason for your trip to the city to her sister. Until I told

Charlotte that she wanted nothing to do with you, but she conceded once she understood the reason for the trip to town."

Phillip walked from the room, calling for Barrington. Once he organised the bath, Phillip headed outside to relieve the grooms of the burden of caring for his horse. He knew Lawrence cared for Charlotte; the relief on the other man's face when he heard Charlotte would talk to him was evident. The trick to fixing the problem now lay with Lawrence.

Charlotte paced back and forth, wringing her hands as she walked. How could she face Lawrence and pretend indifference? His comments to her since he discovered she was his wife were cruel. She knew she was no beauty, but she must have redeeming qualities. Didn't a kind heart count?

Charlotte entered into this marriage without false expectations. The groom didn't even attend the ceremony. But the one thing she didn't bank on was her attraction to the man who was her husband. Lawrence elicited responses from her that, when she recalled them, made her blush with embarrassment. How could Lawrence touch her the way he did if he believed those hurtful things were right?

Phillip said that Lawrence hadn't gone ahead with the annulment. What did that mean? Where did it leave her with Emma? Lawrence had another thing coming if he assumed he could have both sisters.

Mrs Hilderbrand entered the room, carrying a glass and a small decanter.

"Charlotte, my dear, you will wear yourself out if you don't relax. Have a nip of whisky to relax your nerves."

Charlotte took the small glass from her friend.

"I don't understand what he wants. I can't take more hurtful and disparaging comments."

"Charlotte, Phillip will throw him out if he is abusive."

After taking a sip of the alcohol, Charlotte sank into her seat. When the sound of hoofbeats clattered across the driveway, Charlotte knew the time to face her husband had arrived. She heard Peggy answer the door, and she braced herself for the ordeal to come. The door opened, and Peggy spoke.

"Miss Charlotte, Lord Clayhurst has arrived. Do you want to see him?"

"Yes, thanks, Peggy. Can you send in refreshments, please?"

Peggy nodded her head and opened the door. Lawrence walked into the room, and the small parlour seemed to shrink. She forgot how tall he was, but his confident stance was lacking today. Even though Charlotte's nerves fluttered in her stomach, she recognised the tension in his body. The interruption caused by Peggy returning with a tray was welcome. When she could no longer avoid the conversation, Charlotte arched an eyebrow.

"What do you want, Lord Clayhurst?"

"Charlotte, don't do this. We need to talk."

"As your sister-in-law, it is appropriate for me to use your formal title. I don't understand what we need to discuss. Correct me if I'm wrong, but I was sure nothing I ever said was worth your attention. You were too busy berating me for my part in the ruse that my father and I pulled on you. If I remember, I had no charms to appeal to a man, and you declined to bed me on our wedding night. The only time you showed an interest in me, the interest evaporated as soon as your beloved called you. You went from my bed into her arms without a moment's hesitation. I realised you intended to wed her and hoped to bed me. I will not be your mistress."

Lawrence ran his hands through his hair.

"Damn it, Charlotte, that's not what I want."

"Oh? Forgive me for mistaking your intentions. What do you want?"

"It makes me ashamed to admit that most of what you say is true. I knew from the start that you were not involved in the scam. It was so right when I kissed you that night in the library, but I wasn't ready to let your father win, so I hightailed it off the estate. After your sister stayed at the estate for a while, I realised I didn't like her. The thought of being shackled to her for life was terrifying. But I'm stubborn."

Charlotte sat still, and to Lawrence's untrained eye, it appeared as though nothing he said made any impression. Lawrence sighed and continued his explanation.

"The night I came into your room, I would have consummated the marriage if Emma hadn't interrupted us. The first night in the library, you were wearing so few clothes that I found it hard to control myself. When I kiss you, I can't stop. Tell me you don't feel the connection."

Charlotte blushed. She understood what he was saying, but did that matter after how he treated her? No, she didn't think so.

"When you kiss me, you confuse me. You make me shivery and achy. But that doesn't make it right. And after the way you treated me, I'm not sure I want to give you another chance to muddle my brain."

Lawrence strode across the room and took Charlotte by the shoulders. He pulled her close and leaned to kiss her. For a moment, Charlotte froze. Soft lips explored her mouth; the sensation was exquisite. She relented when Lawrence ran one hand into her loose locks and slid his hand to her waist. The man's closeness made her mind fuzzy. How was she supposed to fight the feelings he ignited in her? Lawrence's hands wandered as the kiss continued, and Charlotte felt the heat of his touch everywhere his hands roamed.

When Lawrence broke the kiss, Charlotte groaned. With his hands tangled in Charlotte's hair, Lawrence bent her head to the side and feasted on her exposed neck. Lost to all around her, Charlotte didn't hear the soft knock on the door.

"Charlotte, is everything all right in there?"

They pulled away from each other, and Charlotte straightened her dress. Her eyes had glazed over, and her lips were kiss-swollen. Her hair showed evidence of Lawrence's wandering hands. In a shaky voice, Charlotte answered.

"Um, yes, Mrs Hilderbrand, I'm all right."

"Very well, dear. Call if you need me."

Charlotte sank into a seat and looked at Lawrence. The blush on her face heightened her desirability, and Lawrence forced himself to step away from her.

"So, you can turn me into a wanton woman, but what of the kiss you gave Emma? Does she fire up your blood? Did you want to pursue her further? And how long did she stay with you the night you came to my bed? Did you finish what you started with me in bed with her?"

Lawrence understood that if he wanted Charlotte, he needed to tread carefully.

"The answer to those questions is no. And the last reply is that I finished nothing with Emma. I assumed you saw the kiss because you closed the door, but Emma kissed me, and when you saw us, I was trying to disentangle myself. When I got rid of her, I knew there was no way you would open the door to me again that night. I thought I would catch you in the morning. But the accident happened, and I could not tell you I had changed my mind."

"You couldn't have convinced me of anything, especially after Emma ejected Mrs Hilderbrand and threatened me with eviction. I lay in bed for weeks, hoping it would be you the next time the door opened, but you never came. Why didn't you come and visit me while I was abed? Everyone on the estate visited except you."

"I didn't think you would want to see me, as I caused the accident. If I had let a groom go with you, the saddle dislodging wouldn't have happened. I did not know what Emma had done until I saw Phillip upon my return. Charlotte, I have done everything possible to mess up this marriage, but I want us to work."

"So, I'm supposed to smile and follow your wishes. After all the insults and humiliation from dealing with your mistress and having you parade Emma through the house I restored, you expect me to thank you for a marriage I never wanted? My father never valued me, and neither did you. I followed my father's decree because I decided that almost anything had to be better than how my father treated me, even if you wasn't a nice man. You valued my efforts to restore your property so little that you never thanked me. When I purchased clothes, it meant I no longer had to wear that ugly dress. You expressed shock, then let Emma criticise me for the purchases. The only ally I have had through this horrid time is Phillip, and more times than once, I wished he hadn't been the proxy but had been the groom. And now you want to clear the slate and start again?

"I'm ashamed that I caused you so much hurt. My comments and behaviour have been reprehensible, but the attraction is real. While waiting for Phillip to return, I ventured into the village, where the townsfolk gave me a very cool reception, but I noticed the animals were penned up on the last section of the cropping land as I was leaving. I spoke to Davy, and he explained the thought behind the animal and vegetable gardens, and it made so much sense that I couldn't understand why I hadn't done that before. It suddenly occurred to me that I had done nothing to improve my workers' lives because I lacked the warm heart and genuine concern you have for the people under your care. Please, Charlotte, forgive me. Tell me how I can fix this?"

Charlotte's face flushed. She fidgeted with her hands for a moment. Then, lifting her chin and squaring her shoulders, she said,

"I want a wedding where the groom attends the ceremony. I want a wedding where the people who attend care for me, and after the wedding, I want a husband who beds me without bemoaning my boyish figure or my lack of years."

Lawrence nodded.

"There is nothing about your figure that resembles a boy. I was so angry at your presence that I said the first thing that came to mind. After the ceremony, it will be my pleasure to bed you."

Epilogue

THE SERVANTS DECORATED the house as the cook put the finishing touches on the meal for the reception. The wedding guests comprised people Charlotte cared for; her father and sister were not attending the ceremony. Her only family was her mother. It astounded Charlotte how the change in circumstances had revived her mother's interest in life.

Molly bustled into the room and handed Charlotte a small posy of flowers. She gave a contented sigh as she fiddled with Charlotte's headpiece. Lady Whitely approached her daughter.

"You look lovely, my dear," said her mother. "I wanted a love match for you, and after all that has happened, you have the man of your dreams. I wish you much happiness, my dear."

A knock on the door drew three pairs of eyes. Molly opened the door, and Barrington, resplendent in a new suit, walked into the room.

"Molly, it's time you and I left," said Lady Whitely

When they were alone, Charlotte smiled at Barrington.

"Thank you for giving me away today. My father gave me away at the last wedding because he didn't want me."

Barrington beamed at Charlotte. "Be assured, my lady, that everyone on the estate wants you. It is my pleasure to give you to Lord Clayhurst, my lady."

A brief carriage ride deposited Charlotte and Barrington at the small church that served the local townsfolk. Good wishes and smiles followed the carriage as it approached the church's door. The townsfolk lined the walkway, and the church overflowed.

"Are you nervous, my lady?" Barrington asked.

The smile she gave him lit up her face, and her eyes sparkled.

"Not this time, Barrington. My groom is here; I'm not marrying a proxy."

"Well, Lady Charlotte, may I escort you down the aisle to your intended?"

Lawrence watched as Charlotte and Barrington approached. The beaming face of his butler attested to the fact that Charlotte had chosen the right man to give her away. His eyes locked on Charlotte's face, and he thanked his lucky stars that Arthur Whitely had cheated him. His smile widened as Barrington placed Charlotte's hand in his and stepped back.

Charlotte was pleased to share her big day with the townsfolk and friends, but by early evening, she wanted everyone to go so she and Lawrence could be alone. Tonight, she and Lawrence would consummate their marriage six months after their first proxy wedding. Charlotte found it hard to believe that her life, which Lawrence had upended, was now back on track. Catching Lawrence's eyes across the reception room, she tried to convey her wish to leave. A chuckle sounded nearby, and she turned to see her mother's smiling face.

"Collect your groom and go, my love," her mother said. "I think anyone who knows the history of your brief marriage will forgive you."

Before Charlotte could reply, a deep voice spoke.

"Listen to your mother, my love; she gives wonderful advice. Let's drift toward the house, and then we'll run for it."

Charlotte hugged her mother, and the two not-so-newlyweds headed for the house. As they reached the house, Lawrence lifted Charlotte into his arms. She giggled as he carried her across the threshold.

"You can let me go now."

"No fear. I don't intend to release until we reach my bedchamber. Do you need Molly to help you?"

Charlotte gave a shy smile. "You disrobed me once before. I'm sure you'll manage tonight."

When they reached their room, Lawrence set Charlotte on her feet. As he watched her face, he realised she was nervous.

"Are you worried, my love? Don't worry, Charlotte. I will be gentle with you."

Charlotte blushed, the stain covering her chest and running up her neck to engulf her face.

"My response to you is what worries me. When you touch me, I can't lie still. I know that makes me wanton, but you had better be quick if you want me to lie still."

Lawrence hung his head for a moment and then looked at his bride. "I said horrible things to you because I was trying to ignore my attraction towards you. No man wants a wife who lies still with her eyes closed. Your reaction to my touch is everything I've ever wanted. I want to make you squirm and scream my name tonight."

Charlotte grinned. "Well, my lord, you have my permission to try."

Also by Robyn C Rye

Farnsworth Sisters
Marrying a Rogue
Rescuing Hannah

The Buckingham Sisters
Lady Maggie's Challenge
Layla's Unwanted Husband

The Evans Family
Sometimes Love is not Enough
Still the One
Moving Forward

Standalone
One More Chance
Lady Jayne's Reputation
Third Time's the Charm
Can't Stop Loving You

The Marriage Scam
An Unlikely Match
Searching For You
The Unexpected Suitor
The Lady and the Duke
Starting Over
An Unforgettable Stranger
The Duke's Revenge
The Temporary Wife
Against The Odds
Betrayed
No Good Turn Goes Unpunished
Lady Eloise's Soldier
Lillian's Forbidden Beau
Remember Me
Always Second Best
When One Door Closes
Coming Home to You
Chasing Shadows
Fool Me Once
Deserting Lady Audrey
My Unlikely Saviour
Lies and Deception
A New Beginning
Julia's Second Chance
The Hidden Enemy
The Maiden's Redemption
Miss Elizabeth's Season